SWIMMING
AGAINST
THE
STORM

SWIMMING AGAINST THE STORM

JESS BUTTERWORTH

Orion

ORION CHILDREN'S BOOKS

First published in Great Britain in 2019
by Hodder and Stoughton

3 5 7 9 10 8 6 4 2

Typeset in Mrs Eaves by Hewer Text UK Ltd, Edinburgh
Printed and bound by CPI Group (UK) Ltd, Croydon, CR0 4YY

The paper and board used in this book are made
from wood from responsible sources.

Orion Children's Books
An imprint of
Hachette Children's Group
Part of Hodder and Stoughton
Carmelite House
50 Victoria Embankment
London EC4Y 0DZ

An Hachette UK Company

www.hachette.co.uk
www.hachettechildrens.co.uk

To my sisters,
for adventuring together
and believing that anything is possible

CÔTEVILLE & BAYOU SNAKE

SOUTH LOUISIANA

LOUP GAROU
FOOTPRINTS

CYPRESS
SWAMP

DANGER
DO NOT ENTER

OLD
CYPRESS

MARRAINE'S
HOUSE

MARSH

PETRIFIED
FOREST

MARSH

PETRIFIED
FOREST

ELIZA'S
HOUSE

CÔTEVILLE

BAYOU SNAKE

MARSH

DOCK

MARSH

MARSH

SUNKEN
GRAVEYARD

MARINA

SHRIMP
BOATS

THE GULF OF MEXICO

I saw it one night,
In the fluorescent dock light,
The creature called Loup-Garou.
The beast known as Loup-Garou.

Head of a wolf,
Arms of a man,
Teeth of a bat,
It started to stand.
It grimaced and growled
At the rising moon.

In a guttural howl,
In a horrible croon,
It wailed out its name
To the curd-colored moon:

Loup-ga
Loup-ga
Loup-garou

Loup-ga
Loup-ga
Loup-garou

Joshua Clegg Caffery, *In the Creole Twilight*

CHAPTER ONE
Shrimp

Our land is sinking.

It's disappearing into the water.

And no one knows how to save it.

The thought cuts through my heart as I run ahead of Mom, Dad and my sister, down the thin strip of road to the dock where *Whippersnapper*, our shrimp boat, is moored. At first glance you'd never know that there was recently land where the waves are now swishing on either side of us. But look closer and the telephone poles sticking out of the water and electric wires running parallel to the road give it away. Our fishing town, Côteville, is built along the bayou, the lazy river that leads to the sea of the Gulf of Mexico, and every year more of it vanishes beneath the waves.

'You can't stop me from going with you,' shouts my sister, Avery, tugging on the back of Mom's T-shirt and pulling me from my thoughts.

I can tell from the way she's biting her lip that she's almost in tears. Even though she's younger than me, she's three inches taller. She gets her height from Dad and her black hair and dark eyebrows from Mom. My hair isn't like either of theirs; it's pelican-brown and curly.

Dad removes his cap and runs his hand over his head, exasperated.

Today's supposed to a happy day. My twelfth birthday.

From when we were tee-tiny, Avery and I planned to be a world-class shrimping team, just like Mom and Dad. We learned about the different types of shrimp and how the shrimping seasons follow their life cycles, often closing for months at a time to allow the baby shrimp to grow up. On Saturdays we'd go to the market and stand among the stalls selling crabs, fish and pepper jelly jars. We'd help sell the catch with Mom and Dad, picking out the biggest shrimp for our regulars.

Now that it's my twelfth birthday I'm allowed to go shrimping on the boat for the first time with Mom and Dad.

But Avery's not twelve. She's only ten.

She shoots me a scowl that says, *tell them; tell them to take me too*.

My stomach squirms like it's full of flapping fish. Because the truth is I don't want her to come. We do everything together, especially over the summer holidays, but recently I've been wishing that sometimes she wasn't there too. Avery always finds a way to grab Mom and Dad's attention and just once, I'd like to have them to myself.

'Come here, *chére*,' says Mom, hugging Avery. 'It will be your turn soon enough.'

Mom is the most petite woman in our town. At the market, people often try and prise the shrimp buckets from her fingers to carry them for her, but she yanks them back and says if she wants help she'll ask for it. Or she asks, *do I look like I'm struggling?* as she easily balances a heavy bucket in each hand. Flecks of grey sparkle in her dark curls and a tiny cross on a gold chain dangles around her neck.

'There's a reason you can only go shrimping when you're twelve,' says Dad. He crouches next to Avery and flashes his hand. There are two fingers missing. The skin is bumpy where the top of the stumps healed.

Dad used to tell us they were bitten off by an alligator but a few years ago I got him to reveal the real reason.

'Accidents happen on boats,' he says, reminding us again. 'Remember how my fingers got caught in the winch?'

Avery rolls her eyes. 'Yeah, yeah. You've told us a million times.'

'It's a dangerous job,' says Dad, straightening.

Mom looks at Avery and sighs. 'Maybe we could let her go?'

I want to yell that they can't bend the rules for her. They didn't for me. I had to wait until I was twelve. But I stay silent. Avery would never forgive me.

Dad shakes his head. 'You know it's not just the danger, sweetheart. We're busting our tails out here to make a living. The shrimp season is short. Every shrimp matters at the minute. I can't risk not having a good catch because I'm supervising Avery.'

'I don't need supervising,' says Avery as she crosses her arms.

'Look,' says Mom, pushing the hair out of Avery's eyes. 'Here comes your *marraine.*'

Miss Dolly, our godmother, toddles towards the dock from the house. My Maine Coon cat Monsieur Beau Beau prances behind her, his fluffy tail sticking straight up in the air.

'Avery,' calls Miss Dolly. 'Where is *ma petite amie?*'

Miss Dolly is one of a few elders that still speaks mainly in French. When she was a child, French was banned in her school and now she fiercely protects it.

'I'm here,' shouts Avery, scuffing her shoes against the road.

Miss Dolly spreads her arms wide and joyously at Avery. Even if you've only just met her, Miss Dolly makes you feel welcome.

'You and Miss Dolly will have a nice afternoon,' says Dad.

'We'll be back before you know it,' I say, facing her.

Avery pulls a face at me and sticks her tongue out while Mom kisses her goodbye on the cheek.

We leave them standing on the dock and enter the marina.

There are twenty boats in the marina, all with different names. Beyond them is the bait shop and the trailers raised off the ground on stilts, for the commercial fishermen who come and go from out of town to sleep in.

Mom and Dad's boat has a wooden top and an aluminium hull. It bumps gently against the dock, making the tyres Mom and Dad use as fenders squeak. The shrimp nets dangle from upright poles attached to either side of the boat.

I climb on and breathe in the salty scent of the deck. Mom, Dad and I wear matching white shrimping boots. Mine are squeaky clean compared to theirs. Below me, under the deck, there's a cabin with a bed in the bow. Sometimes Mom and Dad'll spend days out on their boat.

'Do you want to take the helm?' asks Mom.

They smile as I walk up to the cypress-wood steering wheel. Mom and Dad's names are embossed into the grain in gold, dulled over time. A shiny new name glints in the sunlight. My heart bursts with pride. My name. Eliza.

'She'll be yours and your sister's one day,' says Mom, smiling at me.

The thrum of the diesel engine starts and I grip the steering wheel. I guide us down the bayou and on to the open waters, hugging the land. It takes a while to know the waters but I've been studying maps with Avery for years. We've memorised the canals that crisscross the ground like someone snipped it with scissors, and the fingers of land that reach out into the Gulf as if grasping to stay afloat. I feel a twinge of guilt to be steering without her.

I quickly realise that our maps were useless. The coastline is unrecognisable. Where there's supposed to marsh, there's water. The canals are way wider than I expected and some of the fingers of land have disappeared completely, sunk beneath the waves. I look to Mom to check I'm heading the right way, and she nods.

'I'm going to lower the skimmers now,' says Dad. The whirling winch lowers the poles down, so they stick out at right angles to the boat. The green shrimp nets balloon out on either side of *Whippersnapper*, looking like wings, before being submerged into the water.

'Now we just keep her moving,' says Dad. His jaw is framed with stubble and his eyes look tired, but he has a huge smile on his face, happy to be out on the ocean.

'We'll have to find you a good nickname so you can communicate with the other boats,' Mom says, after chatting into the radio. 'Dad's "Fingers". I'm "Tooloolou".'

'I want to be "Turtle",' I say excitedly. There are five types of sea turtle around here and I love spotting them gliding through the water on the currents. Once I saw one of the most endangered kinds, the Kemp's ridley.

I wonder what Avery will want to be. Probably 'Heron' or 'Otter', her two favourite animals. I'll ask her when we get back.

I spot the offshore drilling platforms way in the distance in the Gulf of Mexico.

'Look!' says Mom, pointing behind us. 'A school of porpoises.'

'You go and see,' says Dad to me. 'I'll take the helm.' He sits back and drives with his feet.

The porpoises arch out of the water as they jump and follow the boat. I run to the side and lean over. Reaching down with my hand, I can almost touch them and I feel the spray of their splashes against my skin.

'They came to say happy birthday,' says Dad.

I laugh. 'Best present ever,' I say, and think how even just spending time with Mom and Dad alone has made my day.

After exactly fifty-five minutes a timer beeps and Mom says, 'Let's pull up the nets!'

A flock of pelicans and sea birds flap and dive around the boat as the stuffed nets come up, attracted by the smell of the fish and searching for an easy meal. The birds are so close I have to duck.

The net opens out on to the deck, covering the surface with the catch. Huge live crabs clamber over all sizes of flapping fish, shrimp and bits of plastic. I can't believe how many fish there are. The air fills with the salty scent of them.

'Look at this one,' says Dad, picking up a shrimp and examining it. 'Caught us some good shrimp. See here. We need them about this size.'

I go over and examine the one he's holding, seeing the rainbow iridescence in its scales.

Mom's throwing the crabs overboard. 'If you grab them up from behind their shell like this, then they can't get you with their pincers.'

'We don't want the blue crabs?' I ask.

'Only the shrimp,' says Dad, tossing a fish overboard. 'Everything else is by-catch.'

Mom sorts through the fish, tossing the bigger, live fish back in the water.

I gasp as she uncovers a sea turtle. Its green shell is about a foot long and its front paddle-like arms slide over the fish as it tries to get away. One of its back flippers is bent at an angle; it's injured.

'Better put this fellow back quickly,' says Mom, gently lifting him up and lowering him back into the water.

'Wait,' I say. 'He's hurt.'

But she's already let him go.

'He'll be OK. We won't lower the nets again for a while to make sure that he gets away.'

I stand looking out over the water. How did he even get trapped in the net? I thought my parents used special nets that only caught shrimp?

I turn and see the fish covering the boat. They're dying. And there's not enough time to sort them and throw them all back in the water before they do.

And in that moment my whole world comes tumbling down. I can't be a shrimper if it means hurting turtles and killing fish for no reason. I never knew that by-catch was a part of it, that all those other animals died in the process. Mom and Dad said shrimping was sustainable, that they only go out during the shrimping season to make sure the shrimp are protected from overfishing. But they never said anything about the other animals, and there's nothing here protecting those fish or that turtle.

CHAPTER TWO

By-catch

I watch, horrified, as Mom and Dad toss the dead fish overboard. The seagulls and pelicans flock around the boat in a white cloud, diving into the water and picking out the fish.

'Isn't there a way to save the fish?' I ask under my breath.

'There's too many. It's by-catch. It's just the way things are,' says Mom.

'Do the porpoises ever get caught in the nets?' I ask.

'No, dear, very rarely,' she replies. She glances at Dad. I want to trust her. To believe her and Dad. To be happy that I got to come shrimping for the first time. This was supposed to be the best day of my life. But seeing the hundreds of dead little fish being dumped over the side feels all wrong.

When all the fish are gone, Dad slides the hundred or so shrimp across the sorting table and shovels them into plastic baskets. Mom covers them in ice and Dad lowers the nets again. Each time the sorting happens I get quieter and quieter until at last, after four times, I say I'm tired and we head home.

We arrive back at sunset. The mackerel sky is lit up in bursts of blue, pink, indigo and orange. Avery's waiting for us, swinging her legs back and forth as she sits on the dock. I smile, happy to see her and relieved to be off the boat and away from

14

where the fish died. She's next to Mr Guidry, who's tapping oysters with a hammer to see which ones are good.

'Where's Miss Dolly?' asks Mom.

'Resting,' she says.

'Did you have a nice time?' Mom asks Avery.

She shrugs. 'Tell me everything,' she says, turning to me. 'You have to teach me so that I'm prepared when it's my turn.'

I stumble on my words, not ready to talk about it. I don't know what to say to her right now. Mom and Dad are in earshot too. I can't let them know how much I hated it.

'Well?' asks Avery, picking up a bucket of shrimp and carrying it.

I don't think Avery would believe me, even if I told her the truth.

'It was fun,' I say, hearing my voice come out squeaky and robotic. 'We caught fish too but we had to throw them overboard to get to the shrimp.'

'Go on,' says Avery.

'Where do you want these?' I ask Mom, changing the subject and pointing at my bucket of shrimp.

'This way,' says Mom.

I dash after her, leaving Avery behind me with her bucket. I catch a glimpse of the frustration in her expression.

We carry the shrimp buckets up the dock into town. We pass the bright white water tower, high behind the houses on stilts. I used to pretend the tower was a spaceship when I was younger.

'How many times did you lower the net?' asks Avery, catching up to me.

'Four,' I reply.

'What else did you learn?' she asks.

'Nothing,' I say.

'Tell me,' she says, her temper rising. 'You promised me we'd be a team.'

'I am,' I reply.

'Fine,' she says. 'Be like that.' And she flounces off.

I sigh. I'm not trying to be irritating. I don't know what to tell her when I'm unsure how I feel about everything myself.

Our town has two gas stations, a motel, a seafood restaurant, a church, a grocery store and an ice shop. Mom calls the ice shop the most important place in town. We always need ice. Most of the other shops closed down when the water started creeping closer.

The ice shoots out of a funnel and covers the shrimp. Dad packs up the containers in the back of his pickup truck. 'I'll drop this off at the market now. I'll meet you back at the house.'

I turn and head home with Avery and Mom. Our house towers over the flat land on stilts.

At first we raised our home three feet off the ground. But it wasn't enough. After a hurricane three years ago the whole house flooded. So we lifted it to fifteen feet. First, straps went under the house and were attached to a crane above, like a swing, which moved the house out of the way. It swayed in the air and I was terrified it was going to fall down. We had to stay at Miss Dolly's house in the swamp. Twelve forty-five-foot wooden poles were driven thirty feet deep into the earth by a construction truck. Then they lowered our house on to the poles.

Most of the houses are on stilts here but ours is the tallest. Some are completely over water now. Grace's dad docks his boat under their house, where there was once land.

Inside, our house has one main room where we spend most of our time; it's the living room and kitchen combined. There's no free space on the walls from all the paintings and photographs and Andy, the giant stag head. The walls have wood grooves in many shades of brown from the patches of damp.

I flop down on the couch next to a stack of Avery's wildlife magazines and watch the sky darken outside and the pelicans fly past in a v-formation. Avery lies in the chair opposite, ignoring me.

I think of the fish and hear Mom's voice in my head from earlier, saying that it's just the way things are.

That sentence sticks. Why can't it be any different? Why does that have to be the way things are?

I go to the fridge to get a drink. The chocolate milk is gone.

'Did you drink all of it?' I ask Avery. I know she's done it to annoy me. 'You know that's my favourite. You did it on purpose.'

'Well, you ate all the blueberries yesterday,' says Avery.

'It's not a problem,' says Mom, putting a stop to our bickering. 'We'll get some more of both in the morning. In the meantime, how about I make you two some banana ice cream while we wait for Dad to get back with your cake.' It's so hot in the summer humidity that even though we're mad at each other, we both nod.

I storm into the bedroom, in search of Beau Beau. The room is full of multicoloured balloons and Beau Beau's curled up on the bed with a red bow between his ears, next to a collage that says, 'Happy Birthday, Eliza!'

All the frustration drains from my body.

'Miss Dolly made me do it,' says Avery, but she's smiling as she leans in the doorway.

I run over and squeeze her tightly.

'I'm still mad at you,' she says.

'I know.'

'I found something with Grace while you were out. Something you don't know about.'

'You're just saying that,' I reply. 'You didn't really find anything.'

'Did too.'

'Oh yeah. Well, what was it?'

She chews the side of her lip. 'If I tell you, you have to promise to tell me everything about the shrimping. Don't miss anything out.'

'I promise,' I say, softening.

'I'll show you in the morning. It's in the swamp.'

'We'll go first thing.' I'll have time tonight to think about what I'm going to tell her.

'Deal.' Avery holds out her hand.

'Deal.' I wrap my pinkie finger around hers.

CHAPTER THREE
Swamp

Next morning, Mom waves us off from the dock. 'Don't make me blow the horn and have to come find you,' says Mom. 'There's a meeting at the crawfish boil later.' It's a town tradition that once a month on Sunday we gather together, cook and listen to music. The crawfish look like tiny lobsters. They're laid out on a long table tossed with corn on the cob and potatoes, and covered in spices, lemon and bay leaves.

'We'll be back by noon,' I say. Since I'm two years older than Avery they always say I'm the one in charge. Avery and I dash down to the end of the dock where our small motorboat, *Intrepid*, is moored. I painted the name myself. It's the size of a rowing boat with an outside engine. I lean over the side and pull the cord to start the outboard motor. Avery undoes the knot and steps aboard.

'So when are you going to tell me what you and Grace found?' I ask her.

'You won't believe me until you see it,' she says.

We fly northwards up the bayou. On either side of the river, everything is flat. We're entering the floating marshes full of golden green grass; the last pockets of fresh water marsh left.

There are no buildings or people in sight, only white cranes and egrets dipping their necks into the grasses. After a few minutes, the marshes turn into sugarcane fields. When the farmers harvest the sugar, they burn the fields to make it easier, and a sweetness fills the air that you can taste on the tip of your tongue. A United Houma Nation tribe flag flies on the edge of a town in the distance. Then suddenly, we enter the swamp. The trees grow straight out of the water. Miss Dolly's house is off to the right. We'd often play there when we were little, while she sat on the swing on her front porch watching us. Mom and Dad have been leaving us with Miss Dolly for years while they're off shrimping.

We dock our boat next to the kayaks Miss Dolly gave us and switch to them. It's easier to use them to paddle through the maze of trees, navigating the murky waters.

'It's close to here,' says Avery, pulling up to the land and grabbing the roots of a tree to stop the kayak. She steps out. The swamp is filled with patches of solid ground, some that stretch for a mile and some only the size of a stepping stone.

'This had better be worth it,' I say to myself, hanging back as my feet squelch in the mud; I still don't want to tell Avery about the shrimping.

But Avery hears and calls back to me. 'Just a bit further!'

We jump from island to island over the swamp water. Bald cypress and tupelo trees with swollen bases and tall thin trunks rise from the water around us. Long grey Spanish moss hangs from the trees and grazes the top of my head. Here in Louisiana we have the biggest swamp in the whole of the States. The Atchafalaya Basin. It's twenty miles wide and one hundred and fifty miles long.

The water is a greenish-grey colour today, though sometimes it looks more blue. Mom always says I have the swamp in my eyes, like Dad. Whereas she and Avery have eyes the colour of the trees: the dark brown of the bark.

Ahead of me, Avery springs across to the last island and thuds to the ground.

'Watch out!' she shouts, pointing to the reeds she's just passed. I look. At first it seems that there's only stillness. But then one air bubble surfaces next to a water lily and suddenly I see all the midges, mosquitoes and dragonflies.

And basking in the sun, mouth wide open, is an alligator. Its long pink tongue rests between rows of jagged teeth. There must be at least fifty of them. Its armoured head is almost the size of my body. My friend Huy says they can swim up to twenty miles an hour.

I freeze.

We've been sneaking off to explore for as long as I remember. And that means I've had to find ways to stop Avery from getting hurt. That's why I developed The Swamp Lessons. The first lesson in swamp navigation: Don't Disturb the Alligators.

Especially ones in the reeds. It's where the mothers nest and they're aggressive, defending their eggs.

I glance around me. There's no other route to where Avery is. That means there are only two options. Turn back or jump over the alligator.

'What are you waiting for?' Avery shouts and beckons. 'You'll be happy when you see what we found. I promise.'

'Shhh,' I mouth at her, and glance at the alligator to see if she's antagonised it. It watches me but stays put.

I know she's trying to prove that she doesn't need me or my swamp lessons. A twinge of irritation prickles along my spine but I don't want to be left behind. Nerves stir in the pit of my stomach. If I miss, I could be attacked by the alligator. I back up to the edge of the island to give myself a run-up. I take a deep breath and sprint forwards, propelling myself through the air, over the head of the alligator. Its beady eyes follow me.

I land and thump against the side of the next island. I scramble up the bank, banging my shin.

The second lesson in swamps: Watch Out for Cypress Knees.

They're part of the tree's root network and stick out of the water like knobbly knees. They're hard to spot and can trip you up and hurt you.

Huy once banged his leg so hard against one he broke a bone.

I turn back, checking for the alligator.

It splashes noisily into the water towards me. My stomach leaps and I shriek and dart away from the edge.

Avery laughs as I dash towards her.

The alligator stops, remaining half submerged under the murky water, watching us. Relief waves through my body.

'This way,' says Avery, and she points into the forest.

'We're close to Old Cypress,' I say, recognising the trampled ferns to our right. I realise Avery's taken me a different way from our usual route.

'That's how I found it,' she replies, and she spins round to look at me with sparkly eyes.

Old Cypress is the largest bald cypress tree around. It's our hideout. The tree has a wide base that looks like a giant's leg rising out of the water. It's so wide it takes four of us to hug the trunk; we tried it recently with Grace and Huy. They both reckon the tree's hundreds of years old. There are alcoves to sit and hide in, and cypress knees to balance on. Moss drips from its branches and hides us from sight from anyone outside the tree. We've even tied a rope swing to one side of it.

Today the sun casts shadowshine on the trunk,

the shimmering light reflecting off the swamp water on to the bark. The swamp changes every day in some way. It's never the same.

'We're almost there,' says Avery.

'I wish you'd just tell me where we're going,' I say.

'How about you tell *me* something about shrimping,' says Avery.

I pause, uncertain of what to say to her. Shrimping has always been our dream together. I know it will hurt her if I say I don't want to go shrimping again.

'We had to wait almost an hour before pulling the nets up to get the shrimp,' I say carefully.

'I know that,' she says. 'Tell me something else.'

'Like what?' I ask.

'What was your birthday present?' asks Avery. 'Was shrimping your present? They didn't get you anything else?'

I shake my head no. It doesn't seem like the right time to tell Avery about the engraved steering wheel.

'Liar,' says Avery.

'What?'

'Grace told me. Her dad did the engraving.'

I sigh. I forgot for a second that everyone knows everyone here. It's impossible to have secrets.

'I was going to tell you later,' I say. My cheeks redden.

'You promised to tell me everything,' she says. 'I don't want to show you this any more.'

She quickens her pace, winding through the trees, and I lose sight of her for a second.

'I'm sorry,' I call, dashing after her. She keeps running. 'You want to know the truth?' My voice rises. 'I didn't even like shrimping.'

Her head pops up over a thick fallen trunk ahead of me. 'Really?'

I nod.

'Why?' she asks suspiciously.

I pause for a second then say, 'It was boring. We lowered the nets and waited and then pulled up the shrimp and then lowered the nets and we did that over and over again.'

'I could have told you it wouldn't be any fun without me,' Avery says.

I smile and roll my eyes at her. 'I really want to see what you found.'

A red cardinal bird sings a two-part whistle in the treetop near me.

'Have you told Mom and Dad you don't like shrimping?' she asks.

My stomach squirms at the thought. 'No,' I reply. 'And don't you tell them.'

'I won't,' she says, and climbs and stands on top of the fallen tree trunk, hands on her hips. 'As long as you don't tell them about this.'

'Promise,' I say.

'We're here.' Avery jumps back down the other side of the trunk.

I pull myself up on the trunk and my shorts snag on a branch.

The trunk has been strangled by ivy.

The third lesson: Never Touch Poison Ivy.

I pause. It's too late. There's already a rash on my arm, red and raised. I fight the urge to scratch it.

I let myself gently thud down the other side of the trunk. I notice the base of the stump and the hundreds of rings in it. The tree must have been hundreds of years old.

Avery's a few feet ahead, crouched low to the ground, pointing.

I bend over next to her.

It's a footprint.

But not a normal one. It's giant. Four times the size of my foot. The print is sunk deep into the mud. Whatever made it must be heavy.

A crumpled leaf covers the base and I lift it up. The print has a human shape and five toes.

I kneel down next to it. It's huge but it looks like it came from a human. A giant human.

'Loup-garou,' whispers Avery, and as she says the words her eyes shine with excitement.

My stomach fills with butterflies. 'They can't be real,' I say under my breath.

Avery points to the ground ahead.

There's another print.

I follow it with my eyes, spotting another one just in front of it. The trail leads deep into the forest. I picture a giant human with a wolf's head prowling through the thick swamp, and I shiver.

CHAPTER FOUR

Loup-garou

'Did you make the prints?' I ask her, squinting, examining her.

'No. I swear on my life,' she says. 'Me and Grace found them together. At the same time.'

'Really? You're telling the truth?'

'Five hundred per cent.'

'That's not a thing,' I say. 'Percentages don't work like that.'

'Maybe I meant it metaphorically,' she replies, and sticks out her tongue.

I stare at her quizzically. Avery ignores me and squats to examine the prints again, edging as close as possible without stepping on them. The way her nose crinkles as she focuses her gaze tells me that she really thinks they're real.

'Fine,' I say. 'I believe you. You didn't make the prints.' I rack my brain to figure out what could have.

Was it a bear? The wrong shape. *A giant raccoon?* They do have thumbs and five toes.

But a giant raccoon sounds just as scary as a loup-garou.

Sweat gathers on my forehead. The sun is high in the sky. It's already midday.

'We've got to go home,' I say, wiping it away with my sleeve. 'You know Mom will blame me if we're late.'

'Wait, don't you think the footprints lead somewhere?' asks Avery.

'We'll come back later,' I say.

She nods.

'Here, we should take a picture. Just in case they disappear before we can come back. We can research it when we get home. See if there are any animals that have this kind of print.' I hand her my scratched-up phone and she crouches and takes a picture of them.

We push past the veil of moss and run back through the swamp, flying over rocks and ducking under low branches. I leap across the islands and dodge some turtles gathered on a log. We reach the kayaks and push them into the water, before climbing in.

'Want to race?' Avery challenges me with a smile.

'If you're ready to lose?' My paddles glide through the green duckweed, spraying droplets with each stroke. They knock against Avery's as we both try to get in the same space of water.

Avery purposefully bumps into my boat, making me wobble from side to side.

'That,' I say, leaning forward and poking her with the paddle, 'is not fair.'

But she just giggles and floats ahead, her hair blowing behind her in the wind.

My arms are strong, I've been paddling since I was tee-tiny and I quickly catch up, manoeuvring my kayak alongside Avery's.

'You really think it's a loup-garou?' I ask.

'Why not?'

'Because it's a mythical creature.'

'Did you know that we've only discovered fifteen per cent of the world's species?'

'You're lying,' I say. 'Besides, I don't trust you and your percentages.'

'I read it in a magazine actually,' she replies defiantly. 'Think how big the swamp is; there could easily be a creature living here that we've never seen.'

She has a point. Once you get to the swamp, it stretches for miles and miles. Backwater lakes and canals run through it alongside giant lakes.

'And all the animals and birds around here look like they've jumped straight out of a legend anyway.'

I hadn't thought about it like that before but she's right. The swamp is filled with bright-pink wading spoonbills, pelicans with oversize beaks and jaw pouches, knobbly-skinned alligators and spiky snapping turtles. They *do* all look mythical and prehistoric.

'You don't think someone would have seen it?' I ask her.

'Maybe the loup-garou's shy,' she replies.

I smile at her. 'We'll see if we can find out more tomorrow.'

We follow the edge of the swamp until it opens

out into the bayou, the wide lazy brown river that leads straight to our house. We moor the kayaks and climb back in the motorboat.

I put the motor on the fastest setting. I like speeding down the bayou. It's a good way to feel a breeze in the hot humid air.

I shiver as we pass the skeleton trees, the drowned live oaks that still stand grey and ghostlike. Next to them are lifeless cypress trees, twisted and gnarly. As the land sinks and the sea rises, the salt water travels up the bayous and over the flat land, drowning the oaks and poisoning the cypress trees with salt.

Our boat horn sounds in the distance. Mom made sure she bought one with a tune we'd always be able to recognise: three quick ascending notes. We glance at each other, eyes wide. The horn can only mean one thing.

We're late.

CHAPTER FIVE

Hurricanes

We hurry past the abandoned shrimping boats on the side of the bayou with their rusting hulls, until we reach the newer working boats moored by the dock.

Mom's waiting for us there. 'Where have you two been?' she asks, glancing over my ripped shorts and the mud coating our hands.

'Exploring,' I say.

'No more of that for the next few days. There's a tropical storm coming.'

When she looks away we raise our eyebrows at each other secretly. Hurricane season has never stopped us from spending time outside before.

'Come on, before you miss all the food.' She ushers us to Rosalie's. She's a teacher at our elementary school. Her house is the furthest inland and her yard is the biggest so we have a lot of town events there. It's set up with outside tables and chairs and even has a raised wooden platform for a stage. 'It started a half-hour ago.' Mom seems distant. Usually she'd fuss at us for being late. I shrug to myself and follow her.

When we arrive, Huy's dad and Miss Rosalie are playing the slow rhythm of a waltz on an accordion and fiddle. But no one's dancing like usual. The food lies mostly untouched and everyone is huddled in groups, talking in low voices. Mom weaves between the groups until she finds Dad, and I watch as he wraps his arm around her.

'What's going on?' I ask Avery.

'I don't know,' she replies.

I look around the garden. Everything's green and lush because of the high humidity. I spot Grace's black braids sticking out of her blue scrunchie; she's standing next to Huy, and I weave through the adults towards them. Avery's right behind me and runs ahead to greet Grace. They stand off to the side together.

Huy smiles when he sees me and adjusts his glasses.

Our moms tell us we've all been friends since birth; Avery's two years younger than me and Huy, and Grace is a year younger than her. When I was nine, we decided to form a secret group, The Canailles. But recently Avery and Grace keep getting us in trouble by being late or coming home covered in scratches after exploring the swamp. It's always me and Huy who get blamed, even though we tell them to hurry up or be careful. Last week Grace and Avery caught us trying to sneak away to fish and climb trees without them. Since then we haven't done anything all together.

I'm just about to say something to Huy when everyone falls silent. A couple I don't recognise, dressed in suits, stand up on the stage. We don't often get visitors down here. Unless they come to buy shrimp, crab or oysters.

'They have some big announcement, apparently,' whispers Huy to me.

'Who are they?' I ask.

'They're from Soileron. That's all I know.' Huy's dad works for that oil company, as an oil and gas technician.

'Hi, everyone,' says the woman, introducing herself before continuing. 'You all know the land here is sinking. It's a process called subsidence. With the sea level rising too, Louisiana is losing a football-field-sized amount of land to water every hour. And Côteville is vanishing. Quickly. It's too unstable to invest in saving any more. It's too late.'

A murmur travels through the crowd.

'We know that many of you have worked for us for years and years,' continues the man. I glance at Huy's dad and other parents I know who do land management, administration or offshore drilling for the company.

'We'd like to offer your whole community financial packages to help you relocate,' says the woman.

'But we don't want to move,' says Mr Thibodeaux. 'We have more time.'

'You used to be fifteen miles from the coast. Now you practically *are* the coast,' says the man. 'We're just trying to help.'

There are more grumbles and murmurs from the crowd.

My glaze flits over the worried faces around me and my body tenses. That can't be true. We have more time.

'Do you admit you're partly to blame for the sinking?' Mrs Perry stands and gestures as she speaks. 'All those canals you've built crisscrossing and chopping up the land into bits and pieces.'

'This is not us accepting any responsibility. It is merely a chance to help. You can take it or leave it. But I will say this: the money is there now. It might not be available in the future.'

My stomach drops. 'They're going to let us sink into the sea?' I ask Huy.

'Seems like it. People are really talking about moving,' he answers, looking around at the crowd.

Mom and Dad are whispering urgently together. From the look of shock on their faces they're as surprised as we are. I knew our land was sinking. But I figured we wouldn't need to move until way in the future, maybe even after I die.

Not now.

Not today.

My heart races. I meet Avery's eyes. Hers are wide and scared. I don't want to leave the swamps, our tree, the waterways. No matter what happens, we'll stay here as a family.

We have to. It's our home.

CHAPTER SIX

Accordion

The music has started again and picked up into a lively two-step. It feels out of place. I look to Mom but she's still deep in conversation with Dad, her brow wrinkled and burrowed. The heat is suddenly stifling, closing in on me. I want to get away; I feel like I can't even breathe. I turn and walk out of the yard, my pace getting quicker and quicker, until I'm weaving through the stilts from the houses and sprinting out towards the sea.

'Eliza!' shouts Avery. 'Where are you going?'

'Wait for us!' shouts Huy.

I don't wait. I don't want them to see my stinging eyes. I pick up my speed as I dash past the marina where *Whippersnapper*'s moored. My stomach feels curdled with thoughts about shrimping and losing our land. Nothing feels certain any more. The only thing that feels right is to keep moving and I run until there's nowhere left to go but the water. I reach a giant dead oak and press my cheek against it. I glance around me at the land and the sea and the last of the barrier islands in the distance. They can't let it sink. The wetlands are everything. Our home. Our food. Mom and Dad's jobs. I shake my head. The Soileron people can't be right. That can't be the final word.

'You OK?' asks Huy, catching up with Avery and Grace.

'I'm sick of this,' I say, kicking at the grass.

'Of what?' asks Avery.

'Of not knowing what's going to happen. Of not being able to do anything. All of it.' I stare at the ground.

'Whatever happens, we're in this together,' says Huy.

'We're The Canailles, remember?' says Avery.

'We'll find a way to stay,' says Grace.

I smile because for the first time in a while there's no arguing, no hesitation, no youngest-versus-oldest group divide. Everyone's working together again. We're united in a shared mission.

'Remember this?' asks Grace, and she points to the trunk of the tree, where we etched our names into the bark.

The Canailles: The mischievous ones.

Eliza, Huy, Grace, Avery.

'Members must always carry their talismans,' says Grace, reciting our original code. 'Notebook. Knife. Accordion. Waders. And our mascot is Monsieur Beau Beau the Maine Coon cat.'

I reach into my pocket and feel my penknife. I carry it because it was given to me by Mawmaw, my grandmother, not because of some imaginary secret group code. It has her initials carved in the polished wood handle. I use it in the swamp, for fishing, and on the boats. I slide it out of my pocket.

Avery grins and pulls her notebook out of her bag while Grace unravels her waders from her backpack.

'Well, I left my accordion at the crawfish boil,' says Huy, holding his palms up at his sides.

I know he's just saying that to be nice. Unlike Grace and Avery, he doesn't believe in the talismans any more either.

'You didn't choose the easiest talisman to cart around,' says Avery.

Huy smiles.

We all learn instruments because here there's always music. But Huy is the only one that fell in love with it instantly. The accordion is like an extension of his arms.

'We are The Canailles,' says Grace, raising her hand, arm outstretched. 'And there's nothing that can stop us from finding a way to save our wetlands.'

Avery places her hand on Grace's and they both look at us expectantly.

Me and Huy exchange a glance and reluctantly add our hands to the middle. Grace giggles as we lift them into the air. I wonder how long it will be until they grow out of this too.

The wind picks up the waves and tosses them this way and that.

'I have a plan,' says Avery, and her eyes sparkle.

'Meet me tonight by the dock. We'll need the boats.'

I narrow my eyes at her. *What's she thinking?*

'OK,' says Grace.

'I'll try,' says Huy.

'There's something you need to see,' says Avery earnestly. 'We'll be there around ten.'

'As long as Mom and Dad don't stay up late,' I add.

They nod.

'Bring your fishing rod, Huy,' says Avery. 'And some oranges, Grace.'

As we walk back to the crawfish boil together, we pass the cemetery, with only a few gravestones left sticking out of the water. When Mawmaw died the cemetery had already begun to flood, so we had to bury her in the next town. I remember asking Mom if we could raise it, like our houses, but Mom said you couldn't raise a graveyard up on stilts. It wouldn't work.

We spend the rest of the afternoon at the crawfish boil. After dinner, as the weather gets worse, we head to our house. Mom always says that because where we live is flat and you can see the whole sky, we get the best sunsets. Tonight the clouds form pink and orange fists punching across the sky that give way to greenish-grey storm clouds above us. In the dusky light, bats flit along the coastline and over the water.

We step indoors just as hail clatters on to the balcony outside. Mom switches on the weather report. 'Better keep Beau Beau inside tonight,' she says, and frowns at the swirling white clouds over the Gulf of Mexico on the weather radar on television. 'They've given it a name: Tropical Storm Dorian. They don't think it'll hit the land,' she says. 'But let's keep an eye on it.'

I nod. All hurricanes begin as tropical storms. They come in different categories, from one to five. If it gets up to a category three, we'll have to evacuate. The only category-five hurricane I know about is the one that hit New Orleans called Katrina. It was before I was born.

Mom says the barrier islands, the wetlands and the marshes are nature's speed bumps. They stop the hurricane before it makes landfall. But now with the wetlands vanishing, there's more chance of a bigger storm reaching us.

The biggest hurricane I remember was one called Gustav, which blew the roof off Miss Rosalie's house and left us with no electricity for a week.

Dad's already closing the shutters and boarding up the windows to protect against any strong winds.

We have our emergency hurricane bag that's ready to grab and go if we need to evacuate. Inside is:

Food (cereal bars and cans of beans)
Can opener
Medical kit
Change of clothes
Four gallons of water
All our baby photos in waterproof bags and
    our birth certificates
The photos Mom has of her parents,
    Mawmaw and Pawpaw
Battery-powered radio
Flashlight
Batteries
Sleeping bag
Pens, paper, pencil
Dad's tools
Plastic sheeting
Dust mask
Whistle
Dried food for Beau Beau

We haven't needed the to-go bag yet. But every year we check and update it.

A loose piece of flapping tarp is suddenly still. I look at the treetops. They've stopped swaying. The wind has died down and the air is strangely still.

Mom's phone buzzes a loud alarm. Four long siren tones. It makes me jump. We all crowd around the message that's popped on to the screen.

Emergency Alert.
Tornado warning in your area.
Take shelter now.

'Everyone in the bathroom,' says Mom, ushering us inside. 'Come on. Hurry now.'

I scan the room for Monsieur Beau Beau and spot him lying on top of the fridge. His fluffy tail dangles over the edge of it. His favourite cool spot. I dash over and lift him on to my shoulder. He rubs his cheek against my neck.

'Quickly,' says Mom.

The bathroom is the only room in the house with no windows. I sit in the bathtub and attempt to keep Beau Beau with me too. He's wriggling.

Avery runs in with all our pillows tucked under her arms. She climbs into the tub opposite me and passes me one. This is the second tornado warning already this summer. Mom leans in the doorway watching the weather outside through the front window and checking her phone repeatedly.

'What's the difference between a tornado and a hurricane?' asks Avery.

'A hurricane can be hundreds of miles wide and last for days, even weeks, damaging a large area,' says Mom. 'A tornado is much smaller in size and usually lasts about ten minutes but the strength of the winds can be just as dangerous.'

Avery pulls a notebook from her pocket and jots something down. She's got that look in her eye that means she's up to something.

I can only think about the tornado, and listen out for the whoosh of wind.

I slide my hairband out of my hair and try to distract Beau Beau with it, pretending it's a piece of string. He's not interested. Instead, he meows, jumps out of the tub and paces the bathroom floor.

The last time there was a warning we were sitting in the bathtub for two hours.

Mom's phone beeps an alert again. I clutch at a pillow.

'They've downgraded the warning,' says Mom. 'You can come out now.'

I let my head rest against the pillow and wait for my racing heartbeat to return to normal.

'Good,' says Avery, grabbing my arm and pulling me up and out of the room. 'We've got things to do.'

We tuck ourselves up on the couch by the window overlooking the last of the land that stretches out in strands in front of our house.

Mom and Dad tidy up the kitchen together.

Monsieur Beau Beau weaves in and out of my legs, purring over the thrum of the window-box air conditioner. When we first got him I was worried that his thick hair would make him too hot in the heat here. But Mom assured me that actually his hair is designed to keep him warm in the winter and cool in the summer.

'I think the plan's going to work,' Avery says, playing with her necklace. It's a delicate chain with a gold star attached. We have matching ones.

I sit up, excited to finally hear her idea.

'I've been reading about the American burying beetle. It's close to extinction so the government has saved land and created a sanctuary for it to live. I realised that if they find an endangered species, or a new species that only lives in one area, then they *have* to protect that land.'

'So you want to find a new species?' I ask, thinking back to her pile of wildlife magazines.

'Not just any species.' She lowers her voice. 'The loup-garou.'

CHAPTER SEVEN

Plan

'That's ridiculous,' I say, disappointed. 'You know they're not real.'

Avery's expression crumbles and my stomach twinges with guilt.

'But the footprints!' says Avery, her nose crinkling.

'Those footprints could have been anything. And even if loup-garous were real, and we wanted to protect them, no one else is going to want to save a loup-garou. People are scared of them.'

'Well, this beetle buries itself in dead animals and people are still working together to save it,' Avery retorts.

We both fall silent for a while. I want the loup-garou to be real. I want to find it. I want to believe Avery's plan could work. For everyone's sake. But I just don't think I believe it.

'We have to try and do something,' she says. 'I know it will work.'

I realise there's only one way to know for sure and it's not like I have any of my own suggestions right now. When I think about having to leave our home, panic rises from my stomach into my chest. At the very least it's something to take my mind off everything. In the swamp I feel calm and rooted like the knees of the cypress trees. I can be angry there and the wind will whip up my anger and disperse it among the branches, instead of building and building until I feel like I might burst.

'OK,' I say finally.

Avery beams at me, all smiles. 'You're in?' she asks, her eyes lighting up.

I smile back at her. 'I'm in,' I say, and a small spark of excitement shoots through my body. Just maybe we'll find something that will help.

Avery is convinced loup-garous are nocturnal and we'll only be able to find one at night so we decide to go tonight. Before bed, we secretly pack our backpacks full of supplies. I grab some links of rice-stuffed sausage — boudin — for a snack, making sure we have enough for everyone. At the last minute I add some hot sauce. We put hot sauce on everything in our house. Avery brings her notebook. We lie in the dark, listening for the creak of Mom and Dad getting into bed. When the house falls silent, I switch on the bedside lamp and pull on Dad's rubber waders. They reach up to my waist. Then I thread my arms through my raincoat. I don't want to get eaten by mosquitoes or covered in swamp water. Lastly, I attach my head lamp and fasten my knife to my belt. I'm ready.

'Have you got the camera?' I ask.

Avery nods.

Beau meows loudly. 'Not tonight,' I whisper to him. 'You can come with us next time.' I lift his heavy body up and he pushes his forehead against mine before jumping down.

We tiptoe through the house.

Avery clicks the front door open and we close it softly behind us.

Outside, the air throbs with the buzz of cicadas. There aren't many street lamps around and on a clear night like tonight, stars cover the sky.

'How do you think we'll find a loup-garou?' I ask.

'We go back to the footprints, hide and wait.'

The moon is almost full and reflects in the bayou.

Avery stops at our neighbour's shed. He lets us store our bicycles and some other things in it so we don't have to carry them up and down from the house every time we want to use them. 'Keep a lookout,' she says. 'I'm going to grab some rope.'

I wonder how much rope it would take to tie up a loup-garou.

'Hang on,' I whisper, stepping inside after her. 'We should get the fishing nets too. That way we can lay a trap.'

'Good idea,' she says.

A moving light outside catches my eye.

'Avery,' I whisper, yanking her down behind a four-wheeler, next to brooms and tools.

Footsteps approach.

Someone's right outside. The door to the shed closes. Then the lock slides across and the padlock clicks shut.

Avery dashes to the window. 'It's Tom's dad. He must be securing everything down because of the storm.' The torchlight bobs away.

I rattle the door. It won't budge.

Panic catches in the back of my throat.

We're locked inside.

'We'll have to break the window,' says Avery. It's the kind that slides up but it's stuck, or locked.

'Wait,' I reply, undoing my knife from my belt and sliding it under the window. I manage to lift the window slightly and squeeze my fingers under but the window won't open any further; it's too stiff.

'Help me,' I say to Avery through clenched teeth, pulling with all my might.

Avery slides her fingers under as well and together we heave the sill up, the window jerking open. I hold it while she squeezes out, before passing her the rope and nets, and then swing my body through. I thud down the other side, glad to be free outside again and thankful our mission isn't over before it's even started.

At the dock we meet Huy and Grace. The stars shimmer on the water.

'Did everyone bring everything?' asks Avery.

We empty our bags on to the bottom of the motorboat.

Avery opens her notebook and ticks things off. 'Rope. Check. Food. Check. Fishing rod. Check.' She sits back and surveys it all before folding her arms across her chest, happy with our supplies.

'Are you going to tell us where we're going yet?' Huy asks Avery, but he smiles at me as he says it. We're used to her adventures. 'Has she told you?' he asks me.

I think of the footprints and wonder what on earth could have made them. Maybe it wasn't a loup-garou but some other creature that needs protecting.

I nod. 'Her plan's worth a try,' I say. 'Besides, at this point what do we have to lose?'

As I say the words I think about the shrimping again.

Would I lose Avery if I told her about not wanting to do it again?

Huy and Grace climb aboard his boat, which is moored next to ours.

I lean over the back of the boat and start the outboard motor. It rumbles and echoes, loud in the quiet night. We bring paddles too, just in case the motor stops.

'*Allons-y!*' says Huy. 'Let's go.'

We venture into the darkness, side by side. The bats flitter in and out of the moonlight above us.

It's hot and humid in summer here, even at night. Sometimes the humidity can be stifling, but other times it's reassuring. Like right now, it feels like I'm wrapped up in the heat like a cocoon.

As we get closer to the swamp, I shine the flashlight on the water's surface and see alligator eyes shining back at me. They reflect the light, like cats' eyes, only they have a red tinge to them.

We silently pass them and they leave us alone.

As we enter the maze of trees my senses heighten. Even in the darkness we know how to navigate the swamps like the backs of our hands. We've never explored all of it, but the parts we're familiar with, like the path to Old Cypress, we know well. The swamp sings at night with screeching frogs, rhythmic crickets and the rustle of animals.

'How far away are we going?' asks Grace.

'To Old Cypress,' I say. 'Right?'

Avery nods.

'Look!' says Grace, pointing up into the trees. 'A flying squirrel.'

A dark shadow rustles through the trees above us.

It only takes a few more minutes until we bump against the cypress knees and I know that we've touched land. I jump overboard to heave the boat up the bank. Avery hops out and pushes until the boat's safely out of the water.

We make our way through the swamp in single file. Huy plays a tune as we walk. It calms the adrenalin coursing through my body. We head deep into the forest, retracing our steps from earlier, until Avery reaches the footprint and stops.

'Gather round,' she says as she shines the flashlight on her face. 'This is why I've brought you here tonight.'

Avery flips the flashlight towards the ground, illuminating the footprint.

'You could have told me this was the surprise,' says Grace, annoyed. 'We found them together, remember?'

'What is it?' asks Huy.

'Loup-garou footprints,' replies Avery.

'Seriously?' asks Huy. 'This is why we're here? Those footprints are not real.'

Avery scowls at him. 'They're from a loup-garou. I know it. And we're going to catch it. And when we do, they're going to have to try a lot harder to stop the land from sinking.'

'I'm not chasing some stupid make-believe creature,' says Huy. 'I'm going back to bed.'

'Wait,' I say. 'What do you think made those prints?'

Huy sighs, shuffles towards them and crouches, examining them closely. He holds his own foot next to one. He murmurs to himself then after a while he stands. 'It must be a giant bear,' he says. 'In which case, we should really get out of here.'

I can tell he's uncertain what made the prints and Huy doesn't like uncertainty. 'Don't you want to see if it really is a giant bear?' I ask. 'Wouldn't that be pretty amazing too?'

'Isn't searching for it worth a try?' adds Avery.

'How would we even catch a loup-garou?' asks Huy.

'I think there's going to be three ways,' says Avery, ignoring the sceptical tone in Huy's voice. She opens her notebook and reads off a list she's written. 'We have the net, right? The first way is to lie in wait. We know it's been this way. This could be its route home. If we set up the net maybe it will walk straight into it.'

She pauses to look at us for questions, but no one says anything, so she continues. 'The second way is to lure it with food. That's where the fishing poles come in.'

'You want us to catch fish for it?' I ask.

She nods. 'I think it's pretty likely that a loup-garou eats fish.'

'What are the oranges for?' asks Huy.

'In case it's vegetarian, like Grace. No one's ever been attacked, so there's a good chance it's veggie.'

'Or perhaps there's a good chance it doesn't exist,' says Huy under his breath.

'It might like apples, they're my favourite,' says Grace, and she giggles.

'It would eat something that grows here. And there are lots of citrus trees here,' says Avery.

'I think berries would be better,' I say. 'They grow around here too.'

'We can collect some berries as well,' says Avery, sounding exasperated at the interruptions. 'I'm going to record it all in my notebook.' Avery's always been inspired by magazines about the natural world.

'What's the third way?' asks Huy.

'The third way is to track it and take it by surprise. We can surround it and capture it with the net. The footprints head in that direction.'

I stop and stare at her line of sight, at her flashlight illuminating the footprints disappearing into the foliage. Outside the beam of the light it's hard to see much; there's just an impression of dense growth and darkness.

'Let's follow them,' I say.

And we all shuffle forwards, into the darkness of the swamp.

CHAPTER EIGHT

Footprints

I creep onward, shadowing the giant footprints in the mud, careful not to step on any of them. The others follow behind. After six prints, they end. I search around for more but can't find any.

'This is a good place to set up the net,' says Avery.

She holds the flashlight between her teeth while we untangle the rope.

'Sorry,' I mouth at Huy. I know he's not impressed with our plan.

'It's fine,' he says, and smiles.

'We may as well try, right?'

'Right,' he says.

'We should probably come up with a back-up plan too,' says Grace. 'If this fails then we could make the river flood. My dad says that will build some of the land back.'

I know she's talking about how the Mississippi river used to flood and deposit sediment it had carried with it all the way from the north. The sediment built up the land. But now the river is levied, with tall walls on either side, so it never floods and the land never gets replenished.

'That's a bit ambitious,' I say, wondering where we'd even start with something like that. 'Let's brainstorm some other ideas.'

'You think this is going to fail?' asks Avery, spinning round to glare at me.

'I never said that!' I reply, stopping in the path.

'That's what you meant though, isn't it?' says Avery.

'There's no harm in having a plan B,' I reply, feeling defensive. 'It's smart to have a back-up.'

'Give me a chance first, all right? You're my sister. You're supposed to back *me* up.'

'I am! I'm here, aren't I?'

'You think just because you went shrimping that you have all the answers now.'

'I knew you were still mad about that,' I say, her fiery outburst suddenly making sense to me.

'I'm not mad,' she replies. 'It's just you act like you know everything.'

Her words sting. They're not true at all. I feel like I don't know anything any more. I wish with all my might that I'd never gone shrimping in the first place.

'Boo!' says Huy, jumping out from behind a tree in front of Grace.

My heart jumps.

Grace squeals and leaps into the air.

Huy bends over double and cracks up laughing. 'I always get you, Grace.'

'That,' she says, 'was not funny.' She folds her arms and scowls at him. 'Just you wait, I bet if there really is a loup-garou it will eat you first. You're the biggest.'

'Luckily for me I know they don't exist,' says Huy. He looks to the moon. 'It had to be a full moon though, didn't it?'

I think about the legend that says loup-garous are even more active during a full moon.

Grace rubs her hands together nervously.

'What's wrong?' asks Avery. 'Are you OK?'

'I think we should go home,' says Grace. 'It's so dark, and . . .'

'You've scared her,' I say to Huy.

'Oh come on, it's just a coincidence about the moon. You know that, Grace.'

Grace nods her head. 'I know that,' she says. 'And I'm not scared. Loup-garous don't exist. I'm just tired and this is pointless. We should go home.'

'Now you don't believe me either?' says Avery.

'It's not that. Listen . . .' says Grace.

But Avery's already walking away muttering, 'Just you wait.' She gestures to the direction we came from. 'I'll put the net where we first saw the footprints. You two catch the fish.'

Grace hurries after her.

'You have to admit the footprints are a little weird,' I say to Huy as we set up the rod. 'It's not like people come through here often, or ever, really.'

He nods. 'I guess. I just think we would have seen one before. And even if we do find a way to prove a loup-garou exists, how exactly is that going to save us? The land will still be sinking.'

'But that's the point. People will do more to save the land if there's a creature to protect. Even if the footprints aren't from a loup-garou, they could be from something rare or unique.'

'If only the trees could talk,' says Huy. 'They'd be able to tell us straight away.'

We cast the fishing line where the swamp gets deep and perch on the bank watching it.

'I hope we don't catch a catfish,' I say. Their long whiskers freak me out. I always have the urge to push their mouths together into a puckered kiss, to make them look less scary.

'We'd better be far away when we set this trap,' says Huy. 'A loup-garou isn't the only thing the food's going to attract. We've got to think about the bears, coyotes and alligators.'

'What do we do if we catch an alligator by accident?'

'My dad knows how to wrestle alligators,' says Huy.

'Hopefully it won't come to that.'

'I didn't find any berries,' says Grace, appearing from the darkness.

'Where's Avery?' I ask. 'I thought she was with you.'

'She went a bit further away to hang the net. I wanted to find some berries.'

'You've got to stick together in the swamp,' I say, jumping to my feet and striding in the direction Avery'd gone to hang the net.

'Wait, I'm coming too,' says Grace.

'You too, Huy,' I say. 'Avery!' I shout. 'Where are you?'

I reach where the loup-garou footprints start.

'If you jump out and scare us, I'm going to get you back so hard, just you wait,' I say loudly.

I quicken my pace and shine the flashlight in front of me from left to right, sweeping the area with the light.

'Avery!' the others shout. 'Where are you?'

'Did you see which direction she went in?' I ask Grace, spinning round to face her. My heart pounds.

She shakes her head. 'It all looks the same now. It's so dark.'

I spot the net on the ground and run towards it, panic rising. I pause, trying to stay calm. She's still upset with me for yesterday.

Maybe she's trying to punish me for going shrimping without her?

The problem with being sisters *and* best friends is that you know exactly how to get to each other. She knows how much I worry about her. She's probably just hiding because she knows it will scare me.

Even so, I pick up the net and check underneath and around it.

'Did she fall in?' asks Huy.

Shining the light at the edge of the water, I look for any marks in the earth. But the bank of the island is undisturbed. I grab a stick and poke it in to see how deep the water is. It hits the bottom when the stick is still halfway out of the water. Not that deep. I shine the flashlight on the water surface, desperately checking she's not there somewhere.

It's empty apart from the lily pads and bugs.

'She's playing a trick on me,' I say. 'She'll jump out at us in a second. Just you wait.'

All three of us stand back to back, shining the flashlights around us, waiting for her to reappear. Shadows twist on the water as the moon reflects through the clouds. I listen hard, straining to hear her voice over the cicadas. I think about what I'll say when I see her, how I'll drum it into her head that this isn't funny. But the truth is I don't care if she's disappeared to punish me. I just want her to come back.

CHAPTER NINE

Notebook

'Eliza?' asks Grace after a while.

'Shhh,' I respond, thinking I hear something in the bushes.

It's only an armadillo bumbling out of the undergrowth. I watch it wander away, its armoured body and cute pink nose and ears illuminated by our flashlights for a moment until it disappears back into the brush.

'I don't think she's going to jump out at us. It's been too long,' says Huy.

'Maybe she's hiding,' I say, speaking quickly. 'She did that once before. When she was six she got really mad that I collected more candy than her on Halloween so she hid under the bed for hours to scare me.'

'Let's look for her,' says Grace.

'We'll check Old Cypress,' says Huy. 'That seems like somewhere she would hide.'

'Yes,' I say, turning to face them. 'I bet she's there.'

We sprint over to the tree, holding hands in a line, our feet thudding against the ground. Huy looks back over his shoulder as we go.

We reach the trunk and I grip the flashlight between my teeth so I can climb. My nails tear into the bark as I grasp the knots in the wood. Bats scatter from above. Swinging my legs over the branches, I grab the flashlight in my hands again and shine it between the branches, praying that I see her there, sitting in the tree, swinging her legs back and forth, grinning at me.

'Avery!' I shout. My stomach sinks. 'She's not here,' I say. 'Avery!' I scream again.

The others join in too. The swamp fills with the sound of her name, echoing off the water. If she's close by she must be able to hear us. My voice gets higher and higher in pitch until I don't recognise it and I finally fall silent.

'What if she's not hiding?' asks Grace quietly.

I don't want to think about what that might mean. We retrace our steps back to the loup-garou footprints.

'Let's keep searching.' I start to pick up the net but change my mind. 'We can leave this here as a marker.'

'Good idea,' says Huy, swatting a cloud of midges and mosquitoes away.

'Let's turn our flashlights off for a second and see if we can spot her light,' says Grace.

We all nod and turn them off. Without them it's pitch black. Our breaths are quick and raspy. The clouds move quickly in the sky above us; it's briefly clear and for a second the stars reflect in the swamp, but moments later the clouds come and cover them again.

No gleam from a flashlight is visible.

We turn our lights back on and venture deeper into the swamp, calling her name.

I spot something lying on the ground in the mud and rush towards it. Avery's notebook.

It's open to today's date. Written are the words:

Loup-garou sightings: One.
Evidence: Footprints.

CHAPTER TEN
Evidence

I grasp the notebook and clutch it to my chest, scratching my arm on the spiky razor-sharp-edged leaves of a palmetto plant as I straighten.

The three of us glance at each other.

'Let's think about this logically,' says Huy, striding back and forth. 'If she's not hiding, why would she run off?'

Adrenalin pumps round my body. I can't think logically.

'Um, maybe she thought she saw a loup-garou and chased after it,' suggests Grace.

'Why didn't she call our names?' asks Huy.

'Maybe she did. We might not have heard,' replies Grace.

'How long was it before we noticed she was missing?' asks Huy.

'About ten minutes?' says Grace.

'Enough time to get lost,' says Huy.

We hasten onwards, going deeper and deeper into the swamp, constantly calling her name.

'Let's go back,' whispers Huy after a while. 'We need to get help.'

'You go,' I say. 'I'll stay and keep looking.'

'We can't leave you here,' says Grace.

I storm ahead.

Huy runs after me and takes my hands in his.

'We'll find her, I promise,' he says. 'But we can't leave you and we need to get help. We need more people to search with us, more boats and more light.'

'I keep thinking that around the next corner or the next tree I'll see her. We must be close.'

'Does anyone have a phone?' asks Huy.

I shake my head. I left mine at home.

'Then we really have to go back and get help.'

'Avery!' I scream her name as loudly as I can. Birds fly out of the trees. I can hear creatures scurrying away through the undergrowth. We wait, listening for a sound, but nothing comes. My voice is hoarse and my throat scratchy. I wipe my nose on my sleeve. I don't know what else to do.

'OK,' I say. 'Let's get the adults.'

I leave my flashlight on the ground, lit, so that if she's lost she'll have a better chance finding it.

The darkness of the swamp swallows me. I don't want to leave her out here. Alone. In the dark.

'She's tough,' says Huy, draping his arm around me. 'She'll be fine. Even if she is lost. You taught her everything you know about the swamps. And you're a good teacher.'

His words don't make me feel any better. I was supposed to be looking after her.

We boat back in silence. I keep looking behind me, expecting her to be there, waving at us from the bank. When I can no longer see the bank I face forwards, focusing on what on earth I'm going to say to Mom and Dad.

Avery disappeared.

I lost her.

My heart drums in my ear the whole way home. I try not to picture her fallen on the ground with a broken leg, bitten by an alligator or sinking in the mud. I look to Huy and know he's thinking of all the things that could have happened to her too. And then another thought enters my head.

What if the loup-garou took her?

But loup-garous aren't real, are they?

Beau Beau always knows when something's wrong. He's a cat with good instincts. As we arrive on the dock, he's already bounding out of the darkness to meet us. We race to the steps of my house with him padding behind us. I turn to say goodbye to Huy and Grace.

'We're coming with you,' says Grace instantly.

Huy squeezes my hand. 'We're in this together.'

'Mom!' I shout, pushing the door open. 'Dad!'

They're up and running towards me in seconds. Mom dashes out in a long nightgown with a baseball bat in her hand. Confusion flashes across her face when she sees me. 'Are you OK?' she asks, rushing towards me before hugging me and checking me over.

'What are you all doing up?' asks Dad, bleary eyed.

Our clothes are ripped and my waders are covered in mud and dripping all over the floor.

'Where's Avery?' Dad asks, now worried. He ducks into our room and back out again.

'She's disappeared,' I say, and my voice cracks. I spill everything to them.

'I'm going to round everyone up,' says Dad, leaving before I've even finished explaining.

I hear him banging on doors and lights pop on in the houses around us. The nearest police station is miles away but we have a sheriff who lives here and she can call them for help. Until then, I know the whole community will look for her.

'I told you never to go into the swamp at night,' says Mom as she pulls a T-shirt over her head. 'Do you know how dangerous it is? I trusted you.'

She's halfway out the front door and I go to follow her.

'You're staying here. I'm sending Miss Dolly to keep an eye on you. Your parents won't want you going anywhere either.' She nods to Grace and Huy.

'But we know where she disappeared,' I say, my voice rising as I run after her.

'I know the place you described. You're not the only ones who know the swamp. Remember your father and I grew up here too.'

'Please let me help,' I say desperately, swallowing down tears.

'You've done enough,' says Mom.

My face drops and I gaze at the floor.

She rushes forward and hugs me. 'I'm sorry, I didn't mean that.'

I throw my arms around her shoulders.

'Don't worry,' she says, pushing my hair out of my face and meeting my eyes. 'We'll find her.'

I nod.

And then Mom's gone.

'It's not your fault,' says Grace.

Despite Grace's words, the guilt still burns through me. I was the one who was supposed to be in charge. I let Avery carry out her plan. I didn't think how dangerous it would be. She's my younger sister and I didn't protect her.

All I can think is how the darkness from the swamp has followed me home.

CHAPTER ELEVEN

Help

I watch from the porch as everyone gathers at the dock. Lights bob on the water. The whole town is down there except us and Miss Dolly, who is slowly climbing the steps to our house. She reaches the top and plunks herself down in the rocking chair inside.

'Nothing to fret over, dears,' she says. 'We went missing all the time when we were young whippersnappers and we always turned up.' The chair squeaks as she rocks back and forth. 'I'll make us some food,' she says after a while. 'Let's see what you have in the kitchen.'

I wrap myself in a thin blanket that Mawmaw knitted, tucking my toes under the edge. It's not cold but I still want it wrapped around me. Huy and Grace drift in and out of sleep next to me but I stay awake, waiting for Mom and Dad to return and willing them to find her.

I flick through Avery's notebook. There are some drawings of a friendly loup-garou among other ideas of ways to save the wetlands: restore the marsh, build more flood gates, paint an alligator to look like a new reptile.

Without thinking, I stand and walk into our bedroom. I half expect to see Avery sitting there. It feels empty without her, even though her stuff is everywhere. Most of her clothes lie in piles around the room; some hang out over the side of the chest of drawers. Her school books are scattered across the floor, one shoe on top of her maths book. I pick up and slip on her favourite T-shirt, a green one with a picture of a raccoon's head on the front. I'm wrapped up in her smell — shea butter moisturiser, sun screen and sweat, and instantly feel closer to her.

I remember when I was three years old and showing Mom how I could hop backwards. A new trick of mine. I hopped straight into Avery, who was sitting on the floor, and fell on her. Mom always says how I was so devastated I needed more consoling than baby Avery did. I cried and cried because I thought I'd broken her. I hold my arms close to me and hope that it's the same now, that she's fine and I'm over-worrying. But something tells me this time it's different, more serious.

Back on the porch, I see one light that's bobbing back along the bayou. I glance around me. Miss Dolly's sleeping, snoring gently, with a half-eaten biscuit on her lap. The others are fast asleep too.

I sneak out and meet the boat at the docks. It's Mom. She shakes her head as I leap towards her and into her arms.

'We haven't found her yet. But we will. Dad's still out there looking. I just came back to talk to you.'

In the shake of her voice, I hear all the things that Mom's not saying aloud.

Time is of the essence. She could have hit her head, fallen in the water, broken a bone, tripped into one of the oil holes, been bitten by an alligator or a coyote or a bear . . .

In my head I add *or taken by a loup-garou.*

'I want you to draw me a map,' Mom says. 'I feel like we're going round in circles. I don't want to miss anywhere.'

I'm still clutching Avery's notebook so I flick through to the empty back pages and draw the bayou, the swamp and where the footprints are. I add where we banked the boats and walked over the islands. I can picture them in my mind, can see exactly where we set up the fishing net and where I found her notebook.

'Let me come,' I say, ripping it out and giving it to her. 'I can help. I promise.'

She shakes her head and kisses me on the forehead. 'I need you to stay here, safe and sound. I only want to worry about one child tonight.'

She hugs me. 'Now go back to the house.'

I squeeze her tight before waving her off. I know there's more that I can do. I feel it. I clench the pencil in my fist. I shouldn't have turned back earlier. I should have kept looking. I think of Avery lost and alone and my heart tears. I've always been able to pick her back up if she falls down.

But how can I do that if I don't know where she is?

I draw the map again, adding the land south of here too. I sketch our house and the Gulf of Mexico beyond it. Then I wake the others up gently.

'They can't find her,' I say. 'Mom says that she knows the swamp well but it's been years since she went kayaking out there. And the swamp changes quickly. She made me draw a map.'

'That's not a good sign,' says Huy.

Grace stretches and rubs her eyes.

'We have to do something,' I say. 'I can't stand just sitting here waiting.'

'I thought they'd have found her by now,' says Huy.

'Me too,' adds Grace. Her head droops and she picks at her nails.

'Let's go,' I say, beckoning them. 'We have to.'

I expect them to protest, but they don't. They both just nod gravely.

'I'll grab my bag and meet you down at the dock,' I whisper, suddenly aware of Miss Dolly sleeping on the other side of the porch.

I go back inside and stuff my bed with pillows to look like me so that Miss Dolly doesn't worry. Ripping a page out of Avery's notebook, I write a note and leave it on top of the pillows but under the sheet.

Gone to help with the search. Be back soon.

Monsieur Beau Beau meows as I open the door.

'All right,' I whisper to him. 'You can come. You can help us search.'

I pick up my backpack and sneak out, letting the door shut gently behind me. I dash down to the dock, not daring to turn my flashlight on in case anyone sees me. Even though the chances of that are slim — everyone's out there looking for her.

'Miss Dolly stayed asleep?' asks Grace when I meet them down at the water.

'Yep,' I reply. 'Like usual.'

All the boats are taken except for Huy's motorboat so we clamber inside it together. Beau Beau leaps in too and sits at the bow, with his front paws resting on the rim.

We head up the bayou. Every now and then I catch a flicker in the distance from the sweeping beams of the boat searchlights the adults are using.

'They must be able to find her with those,' I say. 'Unless she was taken by a loup-garou.'

'You don't really believe in that, do you?' asks Huy.

'I don't know what I believe right now,' I whisper.

CHAPTER TWELVE

Navigate

'Let's bring the boat further into the swamp with us,' says Huy as he steers around the cypress trees. 'It'll be quicker.'

He pilots it all the way to where we saw the footprints, steering through the water pathways.

Beau Beau jumps on to the land as we moor. We quickly and silently retrace our steps to the place where I found the notebook.

'Let's try this direction,' I say, pointing and getting a mouthful of mosquitoes. They've got worse in the hours we've been gone and now that we're hot and sweaty, we're tasty targets. I open my bag and search for the bug spray.

'Did anyone bring the mosquito repellent?' I ask as the bugs swarm and envelop me in a cloud. I swat them away but they're still there, biting and itching. I forgot to put my waders back on at the house and my arms and legs are bare.

Huy and Grace check in their bags and shake their heads.

'Come on, let's go quickly.'

'I can't,' says Grace, squirming. 'I'm getting bitten and it hurts so badly.'

I'm annoyed with myself for not bringing the spray. This is going to slow us down, hold us back and hinder our searching.

Grace scratches her arm. I shine the flashlight on it. Her skin's already covered in red welts from the bites. Her sharp nails break the skin and drops of blood show.

I quickly dab it up with a tissue.

'Try not to scratch them,' I say. 'The blood might attract other animals.'

I glance around, racking my brains for what to do, then remember the time I saw a fisherman catching bass in the swamp pat himself down with mud to keep the bugs away.

'Man, they're bad tonight,' says Huy, scratching his arm too.

I reach my hand into the side of the swamp where the mud is sludgy and cool, and slap it all over my body. It sticks to my skin and provides a barrier from the mosquitoes. There's instant relief from the biting.

'Use the mud!' I say.

Huy and Grace copy me.

'Ugh,' says Grace. 'There's something in the mud.' She picks off a worm from her arm.

'I'd choose worms over mosquitoes,' says Huy.

I pat mud on the back of Grace's neck. I coat my forehead in it too but regret it as the mud drips down on to my nose and mouth. It tastes mossy and bitter.

Fireflies dip and hover around the swamp, twinkling like stars above the water.

'Is everyone protected from the mozzies?' I ask.

The mud on my legs is drying, pulling my skin tight as it cracks.

'Yes,' reply Huy and Grace.

Beau Beau meows. I try to stroke him but he dodges my muddy hand.

We hasten onwards, now ready for the swamp creatures of the night.

I shine the flashlight across the land and the water around us, looking for more clues: footprints or broken branches.

'Avery!' I shout, and think about her name and how Mom and Dad named her after Avery Island, an island close by that's covered in azaleas and sits above a solid dome of rock salt. Mom says the salt rock underneath is an ancient seabed and that it's as deep as the Himalayan mountains are tall. There are underground salt domes all over Louisiana, even underneath us here in the swamp right now.

As I'm thinking, I spot something glittering in the ground. It catches the torchlight. I pick up a gold chain and cup it in my hands.

'Look at this,' I say.

'Her necklace,' says Grace, crouching down next to me.

It's the same one that I have. We got them last year when we visited New Orleans as a family. We'd eaten ham and pickle po' boys and were dancing to a trumpet player in the street when I spotted the necklace on a stall. Mom said it suited me perfectly but then Avery insisted on getting the same one as me and Mom had to say it suited her perfectly too. Later Mom took me aside and told me Avery wanted the same one because she looked up to me, but I was still annoyed Avery had stolen all the attention.

I hold it up to my neck to check that it's not my own. Beau Beau pads alongside me. I show him her necklace and he sniffs it. 'We're getting close to Avery now, aren't we?' I whisper to him.

'Maybe Beau Beau could get her scent and track her, like a dog?' asks Grace.

'That's my plan,' I say.

'We've reached the end of the land,' shouts Huy from ahead.

I shine the flashlight in the direction of his voice. He's on a narrow finger of land, surrounded by swamp water on three sides, but there's another island ahead of him, just across a small waterway. The earth on the bank of the island looks scuffed up.

'She could have fallen there,' I say. 'Look!'

'Can she jump that far?' asks Grace.

I nod. I'd never admit it to her but Avery's the best jumper out of all of us. She has longer legs than me even though she's younger.

I look at the distance to the next island. It's probably at least ten feet.

'We need to get over there,' I say, backing up and getting ready to leap. I feel a flutter of relief that she's probably just over there, stuck on the island – followed by a wave of panic that she must be unconscious or something, otherwise she would have heard us.

'Wait,' says Grace, pulling her waders from her bag. 'We won't make it across. It's too far. One of us can wear these.'

I stop myself from jumping. If I don't make it, I'll bash into the cypress knees. Grace is right; it's safer to wade across.

'Do you think it's deep?' I ask.

Huy crouches and looks into the dark water, poking the swamp bed with a stick. 'Follow this line between the two islands,' he says, gesturing. 'It's the shallow part.'

'OK,' I say. It doesn't look like it's too deep. But I know how water can be deceptive.

I hold Beau Beau and wade into the swamp. With each step I make sure I can feel solid ground beneath my feet before I put my weight down. I don't want to suddenly be submerged beneath the water. Even moving slowly, the water quickly reaches my waist. My heart thumps. Everything is different in the midnight swamp; I've never been out here this late before. The wind whistles through the moss. I'm more than halfway across now and I can see the bank where Avery must have pulled herself up; it's clearly scraped.

Why would she be going this way?

Beau Beau digs his claws into my shoulder. He only likes water if it's on his terms.

'Eliza,' Huy says suddenly, his voice tight. 'You need to come back!'

'*Cocodrie!*' whispers Grace.

I shine the flashlight around frantically until I find red alligator eyes staring back. It's in front of me, swimming forwards.

My body is rigid with fear.

'Go!' says Grace.

Huy splashes a stick in the water to try and scare it away but it only creeps closer, its scaly tail snaking through the water. I'm face to face with the queen of the swamp.

CHAPTER THIRTEEN
Howl

I freeze, my body rigid with fear.

Should I go back?

'Eliza!' Huy and Grace are shouting my name from behind me. Beau Beau growls in my arms. Grace lobs stones into the water to try and startle it away. The alligator stays still, watching me and Beau Beau.

I take a step back but there's something inside of me telling me I have to push on, I can't stop now.

I scan the bank ahead. There aren't any reeds, which means it's unlikely the alligator's guarding a nest. That's a good sign as there's still a chance it won't be aggressive. I'm clutching Beau Beau so tightly I'm pulling his fur out. I make a split-second decision.

'Get out of my way,' I bellow, and jolt forwards in the water, spraying droplets up with my feet. I gently throw Beau over the top of the alligator so that he lands on the island. Beau Beau turns back and hisses while I splash the surface with my arms, scattering water everywhere. The gator's tail slaps against the surface as I scramble around it and up the bank. I feel something brush my leg and I yelp, scrambling further up the island. I turn, my heart pounding, ready to fight, but see the alligator is already leaving.

I'm left breathing heavily, crouching on the

edge of the bank. Beau Beau nuzzles me. He's the sweetest cat in the world.

'You all right?' shouts Huy.

'I think so,' I say, glancing at my legs and arms. Next to me, in the mud on the side of the bank, there are footprints. They're about the same size as my feet but the imprint pattern is different to the bottom of the waders.

Avery's.

'She came this way!' I shout. I look beyond the island I'm on to the next one, about the same distance away as the previous. This time there are reeds on the bank of it. I'm not getting back in the water. It's too risky to wade again. My body trembles and I rest my head against a tree trunk.

'How are we going to get there?' yells Grace. 'I don't like the alligators.'

'We need the boat,' says Huy, shining the flashlight into the swampy water.

I remember the route Avery used yesterday to bring me to Old Cypress. There was more swamp water that way. 'Go and get the boat. I think there's a way through,' I say. We'll be able to move quicker around the islands with it. 'I'll wait for you here.'

'You sure?' asks Huy.

'Yeah, I have Beau Beau with me,' I reply. 'Be quick.'

'We'll be back really soon,' says Grace.

My heart pounds as they disappear into the darkness and suddenly I'm alone with sounds of the swamp: the trickle of water, the buzzing of insects and the rustling wind. Beau Beau curls up on my lap.

I reach for Avery's notebook and open it to the next empty page, the one after the map. I need to do something right now to stop my mind from wandering to Avery and what might have happened to her.

I scrabble around in my backpack for a pen. Wherever she is, it seems like the thing she would want is for us to continue what she started. I prop the flashlight to the side and write:

__In the midnight swamp__
Loup-garous seen: Zero
Other animal sightings: Cocodrie
    alligators. Flying squirrel. Armadillo
Clues: Avery's notebook. Her necklace.
    Footprints. Scuffed earth

I flick through the previous pages, pausing at a drawing of Santa Claus being pulled along by alligators. This notebook was her Christmas present along with a giant book about the wetlands.

I remember when Mom would read to me and Avery before bed, and when I got big enough I would read to us both. Avery loved that. It was her favourite. She would ask for me every night.

It was reading together that taught us about shrimp. My thoughts turn to shrimping and how I always thought that I was going to love it.

'Eliza!' shouts Huy.

They're back.

The motorboat engine grumbles as they approach. Huy holds on to one of the cypress knees to anchor the boat.

'See anything while we were gone?' asks Huy.

I shake my head. I clutch Beau Beau in my arms, his soft fur pressing against my neck. I crouch and slide down the bank. With my feet back in the water, I pass Beau Beau to Grace and step into the boat. Huy starts up the motor again and we lurch forwards.

'Everything looks different at night,' says Grace, glancing back. 'We should leave a trail.'

'Great idea,' I say. 'But how?'

'I already feel lost,' says Huy.

'If something happens to us too then no one will know that we're here,' says Grace quietly.

We're all silent for a second.

'Nothing's going to happen,' I say. 'I promise.'

I open my bag and pull out everything in it. 'I have some rope.'

'We can tie it around the trees,' says Grace.

I reach for my knife and divide the rope into sections. We attach them to the low branches that we pass, as we follow the line of islands.

The wind picks up around us and moss floats down and lands on the water's surface. Huy keeps a steady pace, manoeuvring his way between the trunks. He hums a tune and I recognise it from his accordion playing.

'What do you like about the accordion?' I ask Huy, trying to distract my mind from the darkness around us.

He thinks for a second then says, 'That you can play the bass and rhythm. And how it's almost symmetrical but not quite. Kind of like how songs fit together. Listen.' He raises a finger to his lips. 'The frogs are croaking to a waltz rhythm.'

I nod my head in time to them.

'And the cicadas are the top harmony. And you hear that low grunting?'

'The alligators' mating call,' says Grace.

'Well, that's the bass.'

I hear Avery's voice in my head saying it fits together like a sentence. She's always loved words. 'The symphony of the swamp,' I say.

We move slowly through the water, not wanting to miss anything, and I shine the flashlight on the islands we pass, checking for clues. 'There,' I say, spotting something on one of the trees. 'I think it's her hair caught on a branch.'

We stop and examine the island for other clues but it's tiny. It's soon obvious there's nothing else there. I shake my head. That's it.

'At least we know we're going the right way,' says Huy.

'Look over there,' I say, pointing at a light on the surface of the water in the distance. It might be a flashlight. 'Quickly, go towards it!'

'What is it?' asks Grace.

I notice a yellow tinge to the light. It twinkles. I can't take my eyes off it.

'Avery?' shouts Huy. 'Is that you?'

As we get closer, the light disappears and is replaced by more lights in the distance. They reflect in the ripples on the surface of the water. Goosebumps prickle up and down my arms.

Beau Beau's eyes grow big and wild as he crouches and watches them.

I have to find out what they are.

But each time we get closer, the lights disappear and reappear further away.

'We're going in the wrong direction,' says Huy. 'We need to go back.'

'Just a bit further,' I say.

'What if they're the feu-follet?' says Grace in a quiet voice.

I lift my eyes from the twinkling lights and repeat the tale under my breath.

'The mischievous fairies dancing over the swamps at night . . .'

'Leading travellers astray,' joins in Grace.

'Or maybe to treasure,' says Huy.

'Let's turn back,' I say. Although I still feel pulled towards them, the only treasure I want is my sister.

It's Huy who breaks the spell, sharply turning the boat so our backs are facing the lights.

I shiver and wrap my arms around my body. We head back to the path we were on, leaving the lights behind us. 'They were just fireflies anyway,' says Huy.

'They were too big to be fireflies,' I say quietly, glancing at the flickering behind me one more time.

As we get deeper and deeper into the swamp, the little bits of land become less and less. Every now and again we hear the distant shouts of the adults searching for Avery.

'Would she have come this far out?' asks Huy.

'There's nowhere else she could have gone,' I say. 'She must have got so lost in the dark.' I imagine her getting turned around, running further and further away from the areas we know.

When we were younger I'd take Avery to the swamp and teach her about it. About the creatures like the nesting bright-pink spoonbills and the alligators. But I never taught her about the swamp at night. Thinking of her all alone in the swamp now fills me with worry. I try to let the gentle bob of the boat calm my racing heart.

We follow the island stepping stones until eventually the boat bumps against solid ground. There are no other islands close by. She must have gone this way.

'Avery!' I shout as I clamber out, steadying myself on the cypress knees.

Beau Beau waits to see if we're all getting out of the boat, then jumps after us and follows along. We walk in a line, all of us calling her name.

After a while, Huy picks up his accordion and softly plays a slow melodic tune in a three-beat tempo. 'To scare the animals away,' he says. 'Grace, stick close to us. Stop lagging behind. What's with you?'

'Nothing,' says Grace, catching up.

Avery loves the accordion. She was the first of us to learn the two-step and always makes me dance with her and spin her around.

Suddenly Grace grabs my arm, squeezing it tightly. I halt. Through the swamp, I hear something that makes my blood turn cold.

A howl.

CHAPTER FOURTEEN

Legends

'What was that?' asks Grace, still clutching my arm.

'It's just coyotes. The adults probably disturbed them,' says Huy.

The high-pitched quavering cry sounds again.

'Are they dangerous?' asks Grace.

I've only ever seen a coyote sitting on the levee, sunbathing and watching the world below it.

'Not if we leave them alone,' I reply, wrapping my arm around her. The flashlight illuminates Grace's strained expression, bottom lip jutting out and wide eyes.

'We should get a move on,' Huy says, looking into the shadows around us.

'Do you remember the first time we ever heard the story of the loup-garou?' asks Grace.

I know she's talking to fill the quietness.

I nod. We were sitting all together by a fire in winter, with some of Mom and Dad's friends, who played guitars and fiddles. 'We're going to sing a song for you,' one had said. 'Do you want a love story? Or a scary story?'

'A scary story!' we'd all shouted, and we shuffled closer to the fire, our gaze transfixed on his face, which was lit up by the flames.

'This is the legend of the loup-garou,' he said, meeting all of our eyes, one by one. 'A monster that prowls the swamps.' His voice grew quiet as he started singing:

'He's looking for people who have done wrong and evil.
There's no tricking a loup-garou.
He'll see right through you.
He'll spot you with his beady eyes,
follow your scent.
You'll be in your kayak,
or playing in the woods.'

The strumming of the guitars quickened.

'You'll hear the crack of a twig.
You'll turn and there'll be nothing there.
You'll think you've imagined it
and get back to walking.
Then you'll hear a rush of wind
and before you get a chance to look up . . .'

He threw his arms into the air, making shadows, and howled 'AROOOOO!' loudly into the night. The other musicians howled along with him. We shrieked.

'What do you think about the loup-garou footprints?' I ask Grace, pulling myself back to the present. 'You were with Avery when she first found them. Do you think they're real?'

'No,' says Grace shortly. 'I wish we'd never found the footprints. I wish I was back in my bed fast asleep, and that when I wake up none of this will have happened and Dad and I'll cook pancakes for breakfast.'

I smile sympathetically at her through the darkness. I know all about wishing.

'So was it just Avery that believed in the loup-garou,' says Huy.

Grace and Huy sound certain but I'm not sure what I believe any more.

'You know what the best part about that night was?' asks Huy, trying to lighten the mood.

'What?' I ask.

'The smores,' he says.

I smile, remembering the marshmallow-and-chocolate cracker sandwiches we'd toasted on the flames.

'I'm so hungry,' says Grace.

'Me too,' says Huy.

I'm not. My stomach feels sick and queasy. I can't imagine ever feeling hungry again right now.

A racoon scurries past us, making me jump. I glance at its bandit mask. It sniffs around before climbing inside a hole in a tree and closing its eyes.

'That's strange,' I say. 'They're nocturnal. Why isn't it awake?'

'Beats me,' says Huy. 'Another secret of the swamp.'

The land opens out a bit and the undergrowth is filled with palmettos and their spiky leaves. My legs ache as the land turns softer; it feels like walking on mush. Beau Beau yowls as he gets his paws muddy and scratches on a tree to clean them.

I shine the light at the surrounding area. A thin bayou river goes off to the left. I thought we would have found her by now. At least discovering her hair means we're on the right path. She must be close.

'Can we stop?' asks Grace, taking some pecans out of her pocket and offering them around to us.

'OK,' I say. 'Just for a minute.'

I sink down against a tree. A mockingbird sings above me. Only the males sing at night. It mimics the sound of a drill. When we were younger and feeling angry Mom would send us outside and make us listen to birdsong. She said it was a good way to calm down because birdsong is soothing. I wonder how calm Mom will be when I tell her about the shrimping and how I don't want to do it. I don't want to let them down. I've already let them down enough by losing Avery.

I open the notebook, adding another entry, trying to take my mind off the shrimping and Mom and Dad.

Past midnight in the swamp
Loup-garou: Heard
Feu-follet: Seen
Other animals: Raccoon
Clues: Hair

A gentle snoring comes from next to me. I pick up the flashlight and shine the light in Huy and Grace's faces. They've both fallen asleep, resting against each other.

'Wake up!' I shout.

Huy and Grace startle. Huy rubs his eyes while Grace whips her head from side to side, staring into the blackness.

'How can you fall asleep right now? Don't you realise she's out there? Alone? And it's all our fault.' I'm shaking, from the tiredness, from fear, from everything.

'That's not fair,' says Huy quietly. 'We'd do anything to get her back, you know that.'

He looks at me with hurt eyes.

'I didn't mean to,' says Grace, and she lowers her eyes to the ground. 'Please don't tell Avery.'

It twists at my stomach and my heart to see them like this. I want to take it all back, to rip my words out of the air and swallow them back down. But like every stupid other thing that's happened today, it can't be undone. I have to live with it.

CHAPTER FIFTEEN

Danger

'I'm sorry,' I say. 'I didn't mean it. I just want her back.'

'It's all right,' says Grace, rubbing her eyes. She stands and holds out her hand to help me up.

I pick myself up off the muddy ground and take her clammy hand in mine.

Before now we've had a clear path of the way she went, with her footprints, the stepping-stone islands and her hair marking the way she came, but now with the land opening up I'm unsure which direction to go in.

I scour the ground carefully for her footprints until I find one. 'Here,' I shout. 'She went this way.'

Our voices are hoarse and raspy from shouting and calling out Avery's name. I wonder if she'd even be able to hear me over the screech of the bugs and the frogs.

'You should play,' I say to Huy. 'She'll hear that.'

He slides the accordion back and forth, pausing every minute or so to listen out for any sound of her. Beau Beau climbs a tree and jumps across the branches, following us from above.

My thoughts circle back to why Avery came all the way to this side of the swamp.

Was she chasing the loup-garou?

Avery's always had what Mom calls a wild

imagination. Once when we were younger a yellow crop duster flew low above our heads and Avery was convinced aliens were inside it.

'What if . . . What if we don't find her?' Grace whispers.

'We will,' I say fiercely, and stride forward. I can't even think about that possibility.

Tears sting in my tired eyes. I shake my head and wipe my face with my sleeve. The sweat and mud on my forehead drips into my mouth and I spit the bitter taste out.

I can no longer hear or see the lights from the adults. It just shows how vast the swamp is and how easy it is to disappear. I reach up and scoop Beau Beau from a tree branch into my arms for comfort. He nuzzles against my cheek. 'Where is she?' I whisper to him. 'You have to help me find her.'

I don't notice when Grace stumbles to the left of me. But the ground squelches and bubbles as she stands up and I'm immediately aware something's wrong.

'Grace!' I say rushing over to her. Beau Beau leaps from my arms and thuds to the ground. The mud next to her sucks my foot down, pulling it deeper and deeper. I try to yank it out but it's already stuck.

'Everyone stop!' I shout. Adrenalin races through me.

Is this what happened to Avery?

Is she buried under the mud somewhere?

Grace is sinking. She's panicking and struggling.

'Don't move!' yells Huy from behind us both. 'It'll make it worse.'

Grace sticks her arms in to try and wriggle free.

'Don't,' says Huy as she plunges her arm deeper into the mud.

'My arm's stuck now too,' she says.

'Stay still,' shouts Huy.

'GetmeoutGetmeoutGetmeout!' squeals Grace.

Huy grabs a long stick and holds it out to me. I pull myself forwards with it, freeing my leg from the mud.

'I'msinkingI'msinking!' says Grace.

I leap into action and grab Grace's torso, careful to keep my feet out of the sinking mud.

Huy wraps his arms around me. We both pull with all our might.

The swamp bubbles and squelches.

It suddenly releases Grace and she falls on top of us, back on solid ground. We lie there, exhausted by the hugeness of everything. I'm soaking and sticky with mud. Mosquitoes and midges swarm in front of my eyes.

I roll over to get my breath back.

Beau Beau cleans his paws next to me. Then

he moves to my forehead and licks my skin, grooming me.

Grace's lower lip trembles and she whimpers. I reach for her hand. 'Are you all right?' I ask. 'Are you hurt?'

'This is all my fault,' she says. 'I want Avery back and I want to go home.'

Thunder rumbles in the distance.

'Just a bit further,' I whisper. 'I know you can do it.'

'I can't,' she says.

We're covered head to toe in swamp.

'At least the mud'll keep the mosquitoes away,' says Huy with a laugh.

Grace's mouth curves into a smile.

'What if I gave you a piggyback ride?' I ask.

She nods slowly and sniffs.

I let her jump on my back and I haul us onwards, around the sinking mud, following Avery's footprints, until we reach a sign.

Private Property of Soileron. Keep out. Danger.

I let Grace slip off my back and drop to the ground. My arms ache. I brush my hands off on my T-shirt. My skin is wet and damp and wrinkly.

'Eliza?' asks Grace. 'What do we do now?'

All the swampland that belongs to oil companies has signs like this. Mom and Dad warned us that they could be drilling holes or releasing chemicals in those parts of the swamps and to never go on their land.

'This is the only way she could have gone,' I say, glancing around at sinking mud covering the area to the left and a bayou blocking the way to the right.

'What about the sign?' asks Huy. 'What if it's really dangerous?'

'They just have those to keep people from trespassing.'

'I'm not sure,' says Grace. 'Mom says a sign like this means they could be storing gas, or other dangerous things.'

'But Avery couldn't have gone any other way,' I argue.

Huy glances behind us. 'We could have missed something back there.'

'Do you want to find my sister or not?' I say desperately. I want them to come with me. I don't know if I can keep going by myself. 'We've got to be close to the edge of the swamp now anyhow.'

Huy shakes his head. 'The Atchafalaya Swamp is so big you could go for days and not see another person.'

'That's not helping,' whispers Grace.

'We'll go slowly,' I say. 'And be extra careful.'

If a loup-garou took her, it wouldn't care about signs like that. It probably can't read, I think to myself.

'OK,' Huy says. 'Extra careful.'

In the distance, lightning illuminates the sky.

Together we step past the sign on to the forbidden land.

CHAPTER SIXTEEN
Clues

'What do we do if we find Avery and a loup-garou's really got her?' I ask as we leave the sign behind us.

'I think that's unlikely,' says Huy. 'But it's better to be prepared.'

'We don't have the net any more. We should carry sticks,' I say, bending and picking one up. I have my knife in my pocket but I've only used it to chip bits of bark off trees or cut rope. I'm not sure I'd want to get close enough to a loup-garou to use it anyway.

'Maybe the accordion will distract it,' says Huy. 'Or we could use Beau Beau as bait?'

'No way,' I say, folding my arms. Beau nuzzles against my shin as if in response. 'Besides, I thought we decided it was vegetarian.'

'What about a sneak attack?' asks Huy. 'I could distract it while you free Avery?'

'What do you think, Grace?' I ask her.

'We have the waders,' says Grace quickly. 'We could swing them at it to distract it while you rescue Avery.'

Huy nods.

'It's a plan,' I say, secretly praying that it doesn't come to that.

'Wait,' says Grace, looking up at us with wide eyes. 'There's something you should know.'

'What is it?' I ask, spinning to face her.

'Skunk,' whispers Huy, interrupting and waving his arms in front of us.

I bend and snatch Beau Beau up to keep him away.

Skunks are the worst.

'Do you remember when your dad got sprayed?' Huy whispers.

I nod. Our garden used to be very messy, filled with old boat equipment, useless objects, fallen leaves and branches. One day I heard him shout from the shed. I ran out to see a black and white creature shuffling away from under the shed. A skunk.

'Dad?' I asked.

'I'm fine,' he said, appearing around the corner, pinching his nose.

But he smelled terrible. I'd never smelled a skunk's spray before. It's so strong it stings your nostrils and eyes.

He stripped off his clothes down to his undies and threw them in a pile.

'I think it's just on the clothes,' he said.

'It's definitely not just the clothes.' I couldn't help but laugh.

'It's not funny,' said Dad. 'I'm going to smell like this for days.'

That made me laugh even more until eventually Dad was laughing too.

The skunk smell did take days to disappear. It hung around in odd places and out of nowhere I'd get whiffs of it.

'Stay still,' says Grace, pulling me from my memories.

The skunk stops and watches us. Lines of black and white merge with the shadows.

We wait for the skunk to pass us, and then we wait a little more just to be sure.

'What were you saying before?' I ask Grace.

'I thought I spotted a skunk,' she says quickly. 'I was right.'

We hurry onwards. Avery's footprints are more regular, and send little sparks of hope through my heart each time I see them. I walk with my eyes on the ground, craning my neck to look closer.

I squeeze her necklace, which is hanging around my neck next to mine. She's nearby. I can feel it.

We wait until we're long past the skunk and then we rest again. I sit and record in the notebook.

__The swamp in the dead of night__
__Loup-garous: None__
__Encounters: Sinking mud__
__Animals: Skunk__
__Clues: Footprints__

Huy plays the accordion loudly.

'Have you ever thought about being anything other than an accordion player when you grow up?' I ask Huy.

'No,' he says, shaking his head. 'I love it. Why would I want to do anything else? It's like you and shrimping.'

My thoughts of admitting my real feelings about shrimping to him disappear.

'Right,' I say, and sigh as I picture the look of disappointment on Mom and Dad's face when I tell them I don't want to be a shrimper. I imagine them rubbing out my name from the steering wheel and I droop my head, letting the side of my cheek rest against my hand.

'I want to study the Earth like my cousin,' Grace pipes up. 'She's a geologist. Or maybe be a vet, or a teacher like Miss Rosalie . . . I guess I haven't decided yet.'

'They all sound fun,' I reply, wishing it could be that easy for me to change my mind.

Thunder grumbles above us. Raindrops fall, splashing against the ground. I lift my head to the sky and let the droplets land on my face, cooling me down, waking me up, refreshing in the humidity. I shake my wet hair.

Then I see the ground. The raindrops stir the mud beneath our feet.

'No!' I say, gazing at the mud. 'The rain's washing away the prints!'

CHAPTER SEVENTEEN

Storm

'Quick!' I shout. 'Follow the footprints!'

I scramble after the tracks, followed by Huy and Grace, until the rain has turned them into mush and they're indistinguishable from the mud. I stare up at the dark thick clouds covering the moon and the stars. Thinner clouds move quickly underneath. A flash of lightning forks through the sky.

'I can't see them any more,' says Grace, frustrated, scanning the ground.

Huy's pacing back and forwards, studying what's left of the prints. 'She was following this rough path through the trees,' he says after a while. 'This is the direction.' He leads the way.

The wind roars through the trees around us.

I remember the Tropical Storm Dorian that Mom was monitoring. I wonder if the others know about it.

'You can go back if you want,' I say. 'But I'm staying.'

Huy and Grace sigh and look at each other. 'We're in this together,' says Huy. 'We're not going to leave you, all right?'

'We are The Canailles!' shouts Grace bravely and she raises her hand to the lightning and the storm.

'The Canailles!' Huy and I say, joining in for Grace's sake.

We hasten onwards as big rain droplets pound around us. I slip on a wet leaf and the notebook flies out of my hand and lands in a puddle. I scramble after it, sticking my hands in the water to grasp the pages. It's dripping, soaking and covered in mud. But at least I have it. The ink has run but I can still make out the words. 'You'll be back in Avery's hands soon,' I whisper to the notebook, as if the pages can hear me.

'Do you think my mom and dad are out here in the storm?' asks Grace.

'I think all our parents are,' says Huy.

'I hope they're all right.'

'They're adults. They'll be fine. I'm sure of it,' I say, trying to be reassuring.

I remember Miss Dolly and hope she hasn't woken up to find us gone, and panicked.

And then I think of Avery, wherever she is. All alone.

As I straighten up, I hear voices.

'Listen,' I say, as Huy and Grace dash over to me. 'Do you hear that?'

Huy tilts his head.

'It's not just the rain and the wind, is it?' I ask.

'No,' says Huy. 'It's people. It's really voices.'

'Maybe it's her,' I say, wondering who the other voices might belong to. 'Maybe it's Avery.'

We hold hands and run in the direction of the voices. The shouts get louder as we approach. Then we see floodlights shining between the tree trunks and a smell of rotten eggs fills the air.

A small trailer is up ahead. Light glows from the cracks around the door. There are people here and I bet Avery's with them. It's the first real bit of hope I've felt all evening. My heart pounds. The cold metal handle turns easily. It's unlocked and the door flings open.

'Avery!' I scream, bursting inside.

There's a desk with piles of paper and files on it. Shelves are filled with white hard hats, rope and other building equipment. There are no people inside. It's empty. I search under the desk and knock over the trash can. Hope drains from my body.

'She's not here,' I say as Huy and Grace rush in.

'Maybe she's outside,' says Huy. 'There are people there.'

His words spur me on and I dash past them, through the door. Outside, I get a clear view from between the cypress trunks: illuminated by big floodlights I see about thirty people in fluorescent jackets and hard helmets, standing around the edge of a roped-off area about fifty feet away. Some are setting up posts and attaching caution tape. Behind them is large drilling equipment.

Grace darts forward towards the people.

'Wait,' I hiss, tugging at her T-shirt. 'We don't know these people. We could get in trouble for trespassing.' I switch off my flashlight so we can observe from the safety of darkness.

'Do you recognise any of them?' asks Huy, crouching beside me.

'There's that couple from the meeting earlier,' says Grace, pointing.

'Oh yeah,' I say, scanning the other faces. 'I don't recognise anyone else though.' My heart sinks. I was sure Avery was here. Many of the people look worried. One man covers his mouth with his hand. Others shout at each other. One woman stops hammering a post into the ground and points.

I follow her line of sight. It's a giant pond, almost like a small lake, and there's something unnatural about the way the water in it is moving; the current is pulling towards the centre of the lake. Movement to the side catches my eye. The trees next to the lake are blowing in the wind in a strange way. They're upright but seem to be gliding to the side, as if they're being pushed on wheels.

'Look at that,' says Huy, pointing to the trees.

Four trees are being dragged into the centre of the lake by the water.

Grace shrieks.

'Shhh,' I say to her, but luckily her voice is swept into the wind.

'Are those trees moving?' I ask.

'Yes,' they both say.

My knees lock with fear.

Trees don't move.

'This can't really be happening,' says Grace.

We watch, stunned, as the trees continue to glide across the water, seeming almost to float. Once they reach the centre of the lake they start to sink, pulled under the water.

'There's a squirrel in that one!' says Grace.

The trunks are sucked deeper and deeper into the centre of the lake until, in under a minute, the tops of the trees completely disappear beneath the water. The lake squelches and burps as it pulls the ground in with it.

The shouts from the people get louder and more urgent. The caution tape is swallowed up and the crowd backs away.

I gasp with shock. 'It's a sinkhole,' I whisper. 'We need to get away.'

I've heard about sinkholes before. They occur when a salt mine underneath the swamp collapses, pulling the earth and everything down with it. I know that they can be dangerous, not only because of the ground being pulled in with it, but also because of the bubbles of gas released from inside.

'The poor squirrel,' says Grace. 'I hope there weren't other animals there.'

'Follow me,' I say.

'Why weren't we warned about this?' asks Huy, shaking his head. 'It doesn't look like it's new.' He steps out from behind the tree to get a better look, his flashlight still switched on in his hand.

'Hey!' shouts the man closest to us, about thirty feet away. 'Who's there?'

We've been spotted.

'I don't think we were supposed to see this,' I say.

'Quickly, run!' says Huy.

'But what if they have Avery?' I ask, pausing.

'We need our parents now,' says Huy. 'There's too many of them. There's only three of us.'

I clutch Grace's cold hand and we run, dodging the branches that whip in the wind and leaping over the slippery boulders, seeing the world through blurry eyes. My wet clothes are heavy and with the cold wind from the storm they feel like ice cubes.

I glance backwards and see the flash of fluorescent coats coming after us.

'What will they do if they catch us?' I pant.

'I don't know,' says Huy.

'We haven't done anything wrong,' I say.

'Except trespass,' says Grace.

'They're the ones hiding a giant sinkhole,' I say.

'Do you think humans can get sucked in?' asked Grace quietly.

My stomach drops and I stop running. Grace and Huy tumble into each other. I hadn't thought of that.

Could Avery have fallen into the sinkhole?

CHAPTER EIGHTEEN

Hole

Footsteps thud behind us. I check over my shoulder and see flashlights shining through the tall, thick trunks, sending lines of shadows streaking across the swampland. I spot a group of ferns, palmettos and thick undergrowth, and pull Grace and Huy down into it with me.

'Flashlights off,' I whisper.

We crawl on our hands and feet. Sharp pieces of wood splinter the skin of my palm. I crouch in the bushes behind a giant fern. 'Where's Beau Beau?' I ask, and my stomach drops as I realise I left him behind. The last time I saw him was when I grabbed him as we went past the skunk.

I squat, ready to stand and look for him.

'What are you doing?' hisses Huy.

'I have to find Beau Beau,' I whisper back.

'He's a cat. He'll look after himself.'

'No! I'd never forgive myself if something happened to him.' And I realise that I'm not just talking about Beau Beau.

'You shouldn't have brought him with us in the first place,' says Huy.

Grace tugs at my T-shirt.

'You don't understand—' I reply, my voice rising.

'Shut up and listen,' interrupts Grace, yanking at my T-shirt.

Over the building roar of the wind, muffled voices cut through the trees.

We exchange glances. Huy raises a finger to his lips. I duck my head low and focus on the shadows covering the ground.

'PleasebeOKpleasebeOKpleasebeOK,' Grace whispers under her breath next to me. She has her eyes squeezed shut.

The voices get closer and louder until I can just about make out their words.

'They looked like just some kids,' says a guy.

'What are they doing out here in the middle of the night though?'

'Let's check over there,' says a woman.

I hold my breath and pray that they don't come this way.

Thunder rumbles overhead.

Twigs crack in the distance and I let out a sigh of relief. They're past us.

We sit and wait in silence until we can't hear them any more and we're sure they're far away, then I start in the direction of the sinkhole.

'Wait,' says Huy. 'We have to go back and warn the adults.'

'They'll know what to do,' agrees Grace.

'After all this, I'm not going back now,' I argue.

Then, over the sound of the rain splattering against the water and the crash of lightning, there's a yowl. I recognise it immediately.

'Is that coming from my head or do you hear it?' I ask.

'It's Beau Beau,' says Grace.

'He sounds like he's stuck somewhere,' I say. I crouch low and creep through the undergrowth, following the cries.

'Wait for us,' says Grace from behind me.

'I have to find him before he stops meowing,' I whisper, and continue forwards. 'Something's wrong. I know it.'

They say more but I can barely hear them, I'm so focused on finding Beau Beau.

I run ahead as the yowling crescendos and I know I'm getting close. The sound cuts through the noise of the wind and the rustling trees.

Goosebumps prickle up my arms and the back of my neck, making me stop suddenly. I can sense something.

Danger.

Dad always said this would happen. That after spending even a few hours in the wilderness you shake off the town and become in tune with the forest. When you hear that voice inside you, you have to listen to it.

There's a hiss from behind me. I instantly jerk my head round. My immediate thought is that it's a snake, a water moccasin. But it's not. It's worse than that. It's an alligator. This time a female. By my foot is a giant mound of grass piled up among the reeds. I'm standing right next to her nest. Her eggs will be incubating inside. She opens her jaws wide at me, flashing sharp teeth.

I'm too close. I should be backing away but my feet are stuck to the spot. There's nothing I can do but stare at her. She lunges after me, sending my heart pounding. I stumble and trip to the ground, trying to break my fall with my hands. Pain rips its way through my arm.

As I try to stand up to flee, my head spins and I collapse back to my knees. I think I hear heavy footsteps and I'm suddenly aware of strong arms lifting me up.

'Dad?' I whisper, and then everything goes black.

When I wake up I'm lying on the ground, on my back, staring at the stormy clouds above. Pain shoots through my arm. Huy and Grace are bending over me, their faces solemn with concern.

'She's alive! She's alive!' says Grace, and she flings her arms around me. 'I'm so glad you're OK.' Tears pour down her cheeks.

I flinch. 'My arm. What happened?'

'You ran ahead and fell and . . .' Huy pauses. 'I think you broke your arm.'

In that instant, the pain worsens and I reach for my arm. 'What about the alligator? It didn't bite me?'

'What alligator?' asks Huy. 'We found you lying on the ground.'

'Am I bleeding?' I ask.

They shake their heads. 'It's just very swollen,' says Grace.

That doesn't make sense. I know the alligator was about to attack me.

What stopped it?

Beau Beau's yowling sounds close by.

'Can you go and get him, Grace?' I ask, wincing as I try to sit up.

She shakes her head. 'I'm not going anywhere without you. I have to make sure you're OK.'

'Take the waders off,' says Huy. 'We can turn them into a sling.'

I nod and slide them off, all the while avoiding looking down at my arm. I know that if I do, I'll feel the pain way more.

'Can you walk?' asks Huy, fastening the material around my neck in a sling.

I stand and nod. Balancing on Huy, I step forward, one foot at a time, until it feels as if we're on top of the yowling.

'Down there,' says Grace.

We part back ferns and uncover a hole in the earth. A deep ditch that was once used for drilling.

'Beau Beau?' I call.

He meows back.

I lie on my stomach and shine the flashlight around with my good hand. The hole is about ten feet deep and a few inches of water stand stagnant at the bottom. Beau Beau is sitting there, soaking, with his fur all ruffled. As I shine the light into a corner, I realise he's not alone. There's a girl with him too, curled up next to the pipelines.

Avery.

CHAPTER NINETEEN

Birdsong

Avery's covered head to foot in mud. My body shakes as I wait to see the rise and fall of her chest as she breathes. She's asleep. Her hands are scratched from trying to climb up the side and slipping back down.

But she's there. She's real. She's alive.

'Avery!' I shout, my voice catching in my throat. I spin my body around so my legs are hanging over the side, ready to drop down.

'Wait,' says Huy, grabbing my good arm and holding me back. 'You won't be able to get back up with your broken arm.'

'I don't care,' I reply, desperate to be with her.

Avery opens her eyes and stands, blinking in the flashlights.

'Eliza?' she asks, her voice croaky. 'Is that you?'

'It's us!' I say. 'We're here. We're going to get you out.'

There's a thud as Grace lowers herself into the hole.

'Wait!' says Huy, but she's already in the pit.

'Are you hurt?' Grace asks Avery in a quavering voice. She lifts a trembling hand towards her.

Avery shakes her head and takes her hand. 'No. I don't think so.'

Grace nods and bursts into tears.

'I'm fine,' says Avery, hugging her, but I see her body heave with a sob as she grips Grace.

'I'll be right there,' I say. I want to hold her and hug her too.

'I have an idea,' says Huy. 'Wait here. Don't go down there until I get back. Promise me.' And he darts off into the swamp.

'Don't go!' shouts Grace. Her voice is high and shrill. 'We have to stay together!'

But he's already left, sprinting in and out of the trees.

I lie on my stomach and stretch my good arm down towards Avery. I know it won't even begin to reach but it makes me feel that bit closer to her.

'Do you have water?' Avery asks.

I shake my head and wish we'd thought of that.

After a few minutes Huy returns, out of breath and carrying rope.

'Where's that from?' I ask.

'The trailer,' he replies, fastening the rope tightly around the trunk of a tree.

'Do you know how risky that is?' I ask, my eyes widening. 'Did anyone see you?'

He shakes his head as he ties the other end of the rope around his waist, before using it to abseil down into the hole.

When he reaches the bottom, Avery climbs on to his shoulders and he pulls them both up, digging his shoes into the muddy wall to get a foothold.

143

As they near the top, I reach down and clasp Avery's hand with my good arm. There are deep dark circles around her eyes from exhaustion but as she meets my gaze her eyes light up, sparkling. She's out. She collapses over the edge and flings her arms around me.

Fire burns through my arm but I don't care. Avery's here. Her hair's matted and covered in mud. She fits into my arms perfectly when we hug.

'I missed you,' I whisper.

'I missed you too,' she says.

I hadn't realised everything in my chest I'd been holding on to and it releases in a flood of tears.

. Huy disappears back into the hole and emerges with Grace, who's carrying Beau Beau. The cat jumps down and winds in and out of our legs. Avery lifts him into her arms and he purrs.

'What happened to you?' asks Grace.

Lightning cracks in the sky above us. The wind picks up into a steady blow. It whips our voices away into the air before they can be heard.

'Let's get out of here,' says Huy, looking up at the dark clouds. 'We can talk when we get home.'

I imagine Mom and Dad's faces when we show up with Avery and feel a rush of happiness that we'll all be together soon.

We move more quickly over the land now that we're not examining every shadow and nook and

cranny that we pass. Soon we're back at the sign
that says 'DANGER. KEEP OUT'.

'How on earth did you end up so far away?' I
ask her.

'I saw something . . . something like a person,'
she says. 'And I followed it. No people come
here apart from us, especially at night. I thought
it was a loup-garou. But soon I was lost. I was
trying to find my way back when I fell down.'

We glance at each other. It could have been
someone from the sinkhole.

'So you didn't see a loup-garou either?' she
asks us as we walk through the rain.

'No,' I say, taking her hand and steering her
clear of the sinking mud. But I remember the
mother alligator and the feeling of being lifted
up. I think about the footprints and the howls.

Was it a loup-garou?

The howls could have been coyotes. Maybe it
was just the swamp distorting everything.

'But we found something else,' says Grace,
and she tells her about the sinkhole.

We pass the tiny bayou and reach the edge of
the land, piling into the boat. Avery sits next to
me. She clutches my hand. I squeeze it. 'We're
almost home,' I say as Huy starts the engine and
pushes us off into the water. 'We'll be back soon.'

Beau Beau doesn't leave Avery's side, curling
up on her lap as we speed through the water.

'Why are you wearing my T-shirt?' asks Avery.

I shrug. 'I thought it might help me find you, somehow. The whole town's searching for you.'

Avery's jaw drops. 'In the storm?'

I nod.

She rests her head against my shoulder. 'I hope they're all OK too.'

A gust of wind pushes the boat off course and Huy fights to steer it back in the right direction. We bump into cypress knees and tree trunks. Large raindrops pour down on us and hammer against the water.

I grab a paddle with my good arm and use it to try to stop us from crashing into the trees. My knuckles are soon raw and blisters form on my hands from paddling. The rain falls in sheets and Avery holds Beau Beau under her jumper, sheltering him.

Lightning forks and branches through the sky above us in pinks and purples. It's almost dawn. The knot in my stomach tightens as I realise there's something missing.

There's no birdsong. The morning birds are silent.

They know something we don't.

The storm's turned into a hurricane.

CHAPTER TWENTY

Boat

The rain hammers down harder and faster until it's impossible to see in front of us. Avery opens her mouth and lets the droplets fall into it.

'Am I going the right way?' shouts Huy.

'I don't know!' I say.

'Let's shelter for a minute,' he says, and guides the boat under a fallen tree trunk that bridges across two islands.

'Once the sun's up we'll be able to see the markers we left,' says Grace.

Beau Beau swishes his tail from side to side then leaps on to the tree. Bits of bark flake off as he sinks his claws into the trunk and climbs up it. Avery grabs him and tries to pull him down before he goes too far away.

'There's something wrong with Beau Beau,' she says. 'He's acting really weird.'

I look up at the dark clouds. 'I think it's the weather. We need to get out of here.'

I hold my hand out and feel the gusts of wind against my skin. As soon as there's a break I say, 'Let's do this.'

The lightning illuminates the trees and the flowing moss. Behind them, the sky is dark and stormy. Trees slant in the strong bursts of wind. I go over hurricane facts in my head, trying to remember anything that might help us. Most deaths are caused by being hit by things from the wind or by drowning in a storm surge or flooding.

I glance around at all the trees and branches that could hit us and all the water we could drown in. My stomach turns.

The best thing to do in a hurricane is seek shelter.

But what if you're stuck outside?

'There's the trail,' says Grace, spotting a piece of rope flapping in the wind around a branch. 'I know the way now.'

I glance down and see garfish spines arcing out of the water like serpents as the fish swim at the surface. Their ray fins curve as they snake up and down. They're bigger than I knew fish could be, as long as a kayak.

One appears right next to the boat, just beneath my oar. I shriek and drop the paddle. It slips into the water and resurfaces a little way away, bobbing up and down. I instinctively reach out to grab it and pain shoots through my arm again. The boat rocks from side to side. I'm thrown towards the edge, closer to the water and the arcing fish. Everything that lurks beneath the surface flashes through my mind: alligators, snakes and giant fish. My stomach lurches.

'I wonder where the search party is,' says Huy.

Thunder crashes overhead, as if the sky has cracked in two right above us. It shakes the earth and the trees. I scream and duck as lightning flashes around us.

'I read that a whole football team got hit by the same lightning strike once,' says Huy. 'I mean, what are the chances of that?'

'Not helping,' I say.

'Don't worry. The odds of being struck by lightning are one in two hundred and eighty thousand,' says Huy.

'I think our odds just went up because we're directly in a thunderstorm right now,' I say.

A giant bolt of lightning zigzags in front of us. It looks like a man running through the sky. I decide to picture lightning that way from now on, to make it less frightening. The rain stings my skin.

'I'm sorry,' says Avery, burying her head in her hands. 'I didn't mean for this to happen.'

The sudden surge of rain means flash flooding, and on either side of us the marshes are already disappearing beneath the water. Beau Beau yowls, soaking wet.

'We'll be back home soon,' I comfort him. 'Warm and dry. You can have your favourite treats.'

The winds are blowing so hard that it's difficult even to breathe. I tug Huy's arm. 'Are we going to be able to make it back?' I have to shout now, to be heard over the boom of the wind and the waves.

'I don't know.' Huy's eyes glimmer with fear. 'Engine keeps cutting out.' He tries to start the motor again. 'Come on, you stupid thing,' he says at the engine, fighting to keep going.

As the winds gather strength they sound like a whistling train. A branch breaks off the tree above us and crashes towards the water. 'Watch out!' I shout. We cover our heads with our arms.

'I can't steer the boat!' shouts Huy.

Water sloshes overboard as we rock in the wind.

'Everyone hold on,' I yell, as the boat is buffeted back and forth on the water, completely out of our control.

Then all of a sudden the wind and the rain stop. Above us, the full moon shines down, lighting up our muddy, bruised faces.

The air is warm and sticky.

'Is it over?' asks Grace.

'I think it is,' says Huy.

Beau Beau's stopped yowling but he's still cowering in the bottom of the boat. I look around, noticing that though the sky above us is clear, storm clouds surround us on all sides. I realise in an instant that we're in the eye of the storm. The centre of the hurricane. It's far from over.

CHAPTER TWENTY-ONE
Marooned

'We're still in the hurricane. We need to get somewhere safe,' I say. 'We only have a few minutes.'

'Where?' asks Avery.

'I don't know,' I reply. 'Away from the water. It will be safer on land. Let's try and reach solid ground.'

Huy leans over and tries to starts the motor again. This time it works and we hurry towards the riverbank.

'Look!' shouts Avery.

'Watch out!' yells Grace.

I lift my head and my stomach drops. There's a wall of water.

A giant wave.

And it's coming straight up the bayou towards us.

'Hold on!' says Huy.

A storm surge.

It rages towards us, getting closer and closer. The water is dark with white foam gathering on the top of it. There's no time to do anything, no time to prepare or run or hide. There's only time to wrap Beau Beau in my raincoat and grip on to each other tightly.

We hold on and we wait; it's only seconds but it feels like minutes. 'Don't let go,' I say to them. 'Whatever happens. Don't let go.'

And then the wave hits.

The boat lifts up under my feet and my stomach rolls.

We're carried on top of the wave of water. I feel the surge pass under the boat and carry onwards. For a split second there's nothing under the boat except air.

Then we crash back down to the water. The boat shakes from side to side and water gushes on the deck as the boat dips under the river. We're jolted to the edge and smash into each other. I grit my teeth as fear rips through my body.

The boat flips and I'm hurled overboard.

I'm engulfed in water. My arms are yanked by the current. Pain flares through the broken one. I'm still holding on to Avery but her fingers are starting to slip out of my hand. I grasp for them under the water but I'm being tumbled and pulled further away until I lose her grip completely. It's cold, so cold, and dark. I open my eyes under water, blindly seeking Avery's hand, seeing only blurriness. Pushed along by the currents, I feel myself being turned upside down in the water. I stretch out, reaching and struggling to force my way to the surface, clawing at the water in front of me. I try to breathe but a gush of water chokes the back of my throat. My chest grows tighter, like it's about to explode if I don't get any air. But the currents drag me deeper.

I can't, I just can't reach the surface.

I stop struggling and let the currents take control, the water whirling around me. I remember my thoughts from earlier about how people die in hurricanes.

Am I drowning?

I swirl in the current and then suddenly I'm at the surface and there's air. I cough and splutter. My breaths are short and sharp; I can't get the oxygen in quick enough. Water and then pain shoots up my nose and into my sinuses.

Before I can fully catch my breath, a wave drags me back under again. There's a moment, under the water, where the panic clears and I can think. I'm being pulled down further but I don't fight this time. *I'll come back up in a second.*

In another instant my head bursts over the surface and I throw my arms around, searching for something, anything to hold on to. I feel an object and clasp my hands over it. I gasp for breath, my head dizzy. The currents tug again but I keep hold of the object and my head only bobs under the water for a moment.

When I'm above the water again I realise I'm grasping the root of a fallen tree. It's still partially attached to the bank of the bayou and isn't being swept along with the current. I drag myself along the roots until I reach the trunk and heave myself up on to it, swinging a leg over the side of the tree and wrapping my arms around the trunk. I focus on taking slow breaths and keeping my grip, while the water continues to swirl around me.

'Grace! Huy!' I shout. 'Avery!'

All I can see is water. Everywhere is flooded, swallowed by the wave. I gasp as a half-submerged car floats behind me.

Did it come from town?

Is everyone safe?

Other trees, ones that have been completely uprooted, drift past.

My body shakes and I splutter.

A sheet of metal that looks like it came from a building careers towards my tree. I yank my legs and arm in as tight as I can. The metal crashes into the tree, ripping off branches.

'Avery! Grace!' I use the last bit of energy left in me to shout their names as loud as I can. 'Huy!'

I droop on to the log and everything merges into the blue of the water as my eyes fall shut.

CHAPTER TWENTY-TWO

Sisters

I open my eyes. There are bits of grit and sand underneath my eyelids, making tears drip down my face as I blink. My head is fuzzy. Everything's silent, apart from the whoosh of running water. It's daylight and I shield my eyes from the sun.

'Don't move,' says a voice.

I turn my head in the direction of the voice.

'Avery?' I ask. She's sitting on the tree trunk next to me. My body floods with relief. She's alive. She's with me.

'Keep really still.'

'Why?' My voice comes out in a croak.

'Hang on, I might be able to scare it off.'

'Scare what off?' I ask, trying to look at my body without moving my head.

'It's just that, well, there's a giant rat on your legs and I'm worried it might bite you and give you leprosy.'

I jump and see what's keeping my legs warm. A nutria. A big swamp rodent. I squirm and it rolls off my legs and flops next to us on the branch. Under it, I see my legs are scratched and bruised.

'Nutria don't carry leprosy,' I say. 'That's only armadillos. Where are the others?' I ask, whipping my head round.

'I don't know,' says Avery. Her hair is matted and her eyes wide. 'I just got swept up here. I haven't seen them.'

'I didn't mean to let go,' I say.

'Me neither,' she says.

'What about Beau Beau?' I ask. 'Did you see him?'

She shakes her head.

I take her hand. 'We'll find them all soon,' I say.

My head is filled with flashbacks of tumbling under water. Every time I breathe my chest hurts.

I make myself look around again, fighting the panic rising into the back of my throat. I try to piece together exactly where we are. I can't see the tall trees of the swamp or the sugar cane, or the ghost tree cemetery. There are no clues; we're surrounded by water, which stretches until it meets the sky. The marsh with its golden grasses has disappeared completely.

Gone.

I close my eyes and lie back down.

I wonder if our houses withstood the surge.

This will be what it's like if the land sinks and the sea rises.

'Are you OK?' asks Avery. 'Are you hurt?'

'I just need some sleep,' I say. My body feels heavy. I can't keep my eyes open any longer.

'You can't sleep now!' says Avery. 'What if the wave comes back or the storm gets worse or they arrive to rescue us or . . .'

I roll away from her, hugging my knees to my chest.

She shakes me.

'What if no one comes to rescue us and we have to sleep here tonight?' Her breaths are sharp, as if she's fighting back sobs.

There's a splash. I jolt upwards. The nutria has rolled off the trunk and into the water. It floats on the surface, limp and lifeless.

Avery lunges for it but misses and we rock back and forth on the trunk.

'Save it,' she shrieks.

'It's dead,' I say. 'I'm sorry.'

We watch it bob gently away until disappears.

'We have to get back,' says Avery. 'I want to go home.'

After everything we've seen and been through over the night, getting home during the daytime in clear weather should be easy. It has to be. 'How long was I out?' I ask.

'I don't know,' says Avery. 'I managed to hold on to the boat until it sank. I watched you get swept away over here, but it took me a while to swim to the trunk.'

I look around, searching for anything that might help us. I lost my backpack and everything in it. The notebook.

I pull Avery's green T-shirt off my body. I still have my original one underneath. I shimmy along the trunk, resting on my good arm. The other is swollen and bruised in shades of aubergine. I snap off a small branch and slide it inside the arms of the T-shirt. Then I hold the branch in the air and the wind lifts the material, waving it like a flag above us.

'There,' I say. 'Now no one can miss us.'

I survey our surroundings, trying again to work out where we are. The bayou reflects the mosaic of the morning sky. We're completely enclosed by water. Terror winds its way along my bones.

I have no idea what to do now.

CHAPTER TWENTY-THREE

Helicopter

We sit side by side on the knobbly trunk, taking it in turns to wave the flag in the air. The winds pick up again and dark clouds streak across the pink sky.

I think of the alligators and the animals. I hope they've survived the storm, and that the salt water that's flooded the swamp isn't hurting them.

'What do we do now?' asks Avery.

'I guess we stay here,' I say, and turn to her.

'There's another nutria over there,' says Avery, pointing to a mass of fur floating towards us.

I crane my neck to see. 'It's too small to be a nutria,' I reply. 'And it's the wrong colour.' Then my heart thuds as I realise who it might be.

'Beau Beau,' I say under my breath. Beau Beau looks tee-tiny with his hair wet and stuck to his body. He's half his usual size.

I pass Avery the flag and slide into the water. I doggy-paddle with one arm towards the animal, pain burning through my hurt forearm into my shoulder.

'Wait,' shouts Avery. 'Don't leave me!'

'I'm coming back,' I say. 'It's OK. I just have to check if it's Beau Beau.'

But in my heart I already know that it's him.

I tread water as I get near to him, freeing up my arm.

I reach the cat and scoop him close to my body, then manoeuvre him over my shoulder. His body's warm. That means he's alive. It has to.

I kick my legs to get back to the tree trunk.

'I'm here,' I whisper to him. 'It's me, Eliza.'

Avery lifts Beau Beau from my shoulders and I pull myself up on to the trunk.

I sit next to him and stroke his straggly hair. 'You'll be fine, Monsieur,' I say, gently comforting him. 'You've got to be OK.'

Avery removes her sweatshirt and wraps it around him. She makes soft soothing sounds.

I place my hand on his ribs and feel a very slight rise of his chest. His heart races.

'He's breathing,' I say.

I remember the day we got Beau Beau. I found him near the dumpster in town all alone. When I approached he rolled over on his back, wanting his tummy rubbed. As soon as I brought him home he drank from the water faucet before jumping up on Dad's armchair.

'Excuse me, Monsieur,' Dad had said jokingly, trying to push him away, but Beau Beau had already curled up in the one bit of space left next to Dad. And he was purring softly. He was the perfect fit.

'I guess he's staying,' Dad had said.

Then Avery and I squeezed each other's hands. We knew he'd fall for him.

In the distance there's a rumble and for a split second I think it's another storm surge.

'Listen,' I say.

Avery's eyes light up. 'A boat!'

My body relaxes, thankful it's not another wave.

I kiss Beau Beau on the head and carefully stand up on the trunk, sticking my arm out to balance.

'Pass me the flag,' I say to her.

She hands it to me and I hold it as high as I can above my head, waving it from side to side.

I keep signalling with the flag as the noise gets closer, even though fiery pain shoots through my arms.

But it's not a boat. It's a helicopter. It's in the distance, too far away to see us.

'Help!' I shout with all my might.

'Help!' screams Avery, throwing her arms above her head and shaking her hands at it. 'We're down here!'

But the helicopter chops across the sky ahead until it's out of sight. My heart sinks.

'We're never gonna get rescued, are we?' asks Avery. 'No one knows where we are.'

'They'll be searching for us. They'll find us, don't worry.'

'I hope so,' says Avery, but she doesn't look convinced.

'I was worried I'd never find you again, but I did,' I say, trying to be comforting. A surge of emotion rises to my throat. 'I was terrified when you disappeared,' I whisper.

'I'm sorry,' Avery replies.

'I feel like I have to be the responsible one all the time. To make sure you're not home late, don't get hurt or lost.'

She opens her mouth to disagree but closes it and chews her bottom lip instead. After a while she says, 'I guess I did run after that person thinking it was a loup-garou without telling anyone.'

Avery's words fill my chest with lightness.

'But you made me feel like I had to prove myself,' she continues, rocking her legs back and forth, sending water spraying. 'Going shrimping without me and sneaking off with Huy to climb trees. I know sometimes I do things without thinking but it's only because you've already done everything I want to do and I have to prove that I can do it just as well.'

I start to say that she doesn't *have* to do anything but stop myself. I've never thought of it like that before, from her point of view. 'I guess I do get to do everything first,' I say. 'Maybe we can be more of a team from now on?'

She grins at me and I smile back.

'Were you telling the truth about hating shrimping?' she asks.

I sigh and gaze out at the water. 'I didn't know that so many fish die in the process. And turtles too. I can't be a part of that. I don't want to be shrimper.' As I say the words aloud, I feel the calmest I've felt since my birthday.

'Well, I don't want to be a shrimper if you're not doing it.'

I laugh and pull her close to me. She places her head on my shoulder and I let my cheek rest against her hair. We sit and watch a dark cloud shaped like a heron morph into a puffy fish. A dragonfly zooms across the water in a flash of blue. Even though we still haven't been rescued, I'm grateful for this moment with Avery.

'A boat!' shouts Avery.

This time she's right. An old fibreglass canoe bobs towards us. Parts of the hull have splintered off but it's still floating.

I lean forwards, trying to reach the side of it as it floats past our trunk. 'Ouch!' I cry, as my arm shudders in pain. The injury's getting worse.

'I can swim to it,' Avery says. 'I have two arms.'

'No, Avery. Don't you dare. You don't know how strong the current is.'

I stretch out to stop her and hold her back.

'We're saved if we get that boat.' She turns and beams at me before she slips into the water.

CHAPTER TWENTY-FOUR
Swimming

The water splashes and she dunks under.

'Avery!' I shout. My mouth is dry and my lips chapped.

She surfaces and front-crawls towards the canoe. I clasp my hands together, willing her to make it.

'You've got it!' I say, as she reaches the canoe.

She pushes the boat, kicking with her legs to propel it forward.

'You've got tears in your eyes?' she questions, surprised, as she reaches me.

'Well, yeah. That will be the third time I've thought I might lose you tonight.' But I smile at her as I say it.

'Now we can find Grace and Huy,' she says.

I break off branches from our trunk to use as paddles.

'You get in first. I'll pass you Beau Beau,' says Avery.

We bring the flag and set forth to rescue Grace and Huy.

'*Allons-y!*' I say. 'Let's go.'

But the branches hardly work as paddles. There's not enough surface on them to push against the water and the current carries the boat.

'I'll kick-paddle us,' says Avery, jumping in the water.

'We don't know how far away Huy and Grace are,' I say.

'Look, it's my fault they're out there. I can't leave them. We're The Canailles. We're in this together.'

I'm about to stop her but realise this is Avery trying to be responsible. 'We'll take it in turns to kick,' I say instead.

'Can you do me a favour?' she asks.

'Anything.'

'Just tell me if you see any alligators.'

'Don't worry. I'm on it.'

But there doesn't seem to be the same amount of wildlife as before. No alligators, but also no ibis, herons, egrets or turtles.

Avery splashes frantically with her legs but we move at a snail's pace through the debris-filled water. Trees have been knocked down and are floating among a sea of leaves and branches.

I spot something yellow bobbing in the water, the same yellow as Grace's coat. I lift it out with a branch and feel my stomach sink. It *is* her coat, dripping and ripped. We turn and look at each other. If her coat's here, where's Grace?

'Grace!' I shout, my voice shrill.

'Huy!' shouts Avery.

'Listen,' I say. 'I hear something.'

There's a faint tapping in the distance.

We follow the sound. It gets louder and louder until I see what's making the noise. Huy's lying over a huge tree trunk, banging a stone against a washed-up clam shell.

I gasp. He's holding Grace.

'They're there!' I say, and I slide into the water next to Avery and help her thrust the boat forwards. Pain shoots through my arm but I hardly feel it because we've found them. And that's all that matters right now.

'You made it,' says Huy when we pull up alongside him. His voice is raspy and quiet. Somehow he still has his glasses on but they're bent and missing an arm.

'Is she all right?' I ask. 'Has she been knocked out?'

'She's OK. I was just letting her sleep. I said I'd stay awake so she didn't slip back into the water.'

Grace stirs, then opens her eyes and beams at us. Her braids have come loose from her scrunchie and are tangled up. She's covered in red mosquito bites. She throws her arms around me and I squeeze her back. Avery and Huy join in the group hug. Now that we've all found each other and we're all safe, my body shakes from exhaustion and relief.

'You stink,' say Huy to me, smiling.

I laugh. 'You don't smell so great either.'

'Let's get everyone on the boat and go home,' I say. The sun's still low in the sky but it's already beating down on us.

Huy and Grace clamber on board the canoe and Avery holds it steady.

'There's some driftwood we could use as a paddle over there,' says Huy, pointing behind the fallen trunk. 'It's flat. It might work.'

The canoe bangs against the tree as we try and push it close enough for Huy to reach back and grab the piece of driftwood. It squeaks against the side as Huy yanks it aboard. 'It's heavy,' he says.

'There's water in the canoe!' shouts Grace suddenly.

'Where's it coming from?' I ask, frowning and trying to peer into the bottom of the boat.

'Scoop it out!' says Avery.

'There's too much!' Grace says, splashing water out of the boat. 'It's filling up fast!'

'There must be a leak,' I say, feeling around the outside of the boat as I tread water. It's mostly smooth with some weeds stuck to it. 'Which side of the canoe is the water coming from? Can you find it?'

She reaches in with her hands and feels around, but shakes her head.

'Save Beau Beau!' I say. 'Pass him to me.'

I lay him over my shoulders and neck.

'We've got to get out!' says Huy, jumping off the boat. Water sprays. 'Can we flip the canoe and save it?'

The back of the canoe sinks beneath the water. For a split second I try to hold it up but the weight is too much. A fiery pain spreads up my arm and I'm out of breath and spluttering from swimming.

'Get out of there!' I say to Grace before she's pulled under with the canoe.

Grace slides into the water and helps us try to lift the canoe. But with nothing to ground our feet on it's impossible. Grace ducks beneath the water and resurfaces, coughing.

Huy grips the last corner of the canoe with white knuckles. His teeth are clenched. 'This is how we get home. We can't let it sink.'

But even as he says it, the last edge disappears beneath the water and bubbles rise to the surface. We all clamber on to Huy's tree trunk together, stranded once again. It's just long enough for four of us to sit side by side. Mud and scraggly roots cling to the base of it. Beau Beau's wrapped around my shoulders. I can barely feel him breathing.

I kick at the water, deflated. After all that, we don't even have a way to get home.

CHAPTER TWENTY-FIVE

Hunger

The clouds clear and the sun beams down, quickly drying our dripping clothes and hair.

Grace tugs on my sleeve. 'I want to go home. I want to see Mom and Dad. I'm hot and scared and tired.' She puffs out her bottom lip.

'I know,' I say. 'When was the last time any of us ate anything?'

'I'm so hungry I could eat an alligator,' says Huy.

'I could eat a whole king cake,' says Avery.

'Now, that sounds good,' I say. The thought of a round king cake covered in purple, yellow and green sugar makes my mouth water.

'I could eat two of those,' says Grace.

'What about a worm?' I ask. 'There's a few here in the mud.' I watch a worm wriggle and hide under the last of the soil stuck to the roots of the tree.

Huy sits up. 'I'll try it.'

'Oh you can't!' says Grace.

'I've got to,' says Huy. 'I have to eat something.'

'Imagine it's a baby crawfish,' I say.

Huy traps a worm in between his finger and thumb. Its ends squirm and slime runs down his finger. He closes his eyes. 'It's just a crawfish,' he repeats before raising his hand to his mouth and dropping it on to his tongue.

He does five quick chews, screwing his face up, and then gulps. He opens his eyes.

'What was it like?' I ask.

'Mmm,' he croaks. 'Delicious. Your turn.'

I know he's lying but I'm so hungry it feels like my stomach's eating itself. 'I'm going to try one.' I place a worm on the palm of my hand. 'I'm sorry,' I say to it, before letting it fall into my mouth.

'Oh my God, oh my God,' I say, squealing.

'Swallow it,' says Huy.

The worm twists and turns. I taste soil. I pinch my nose and clamp my jaws together. The worm goes squelch. I manage three more chews and then swallow it as quickly as I can. It slides down the back of my throat and activates my gag reflex.

I open my eyes to their horrified faces staring at me.

'That,' I say, 'was disgusting.'

'There's not even any clean water to wash it down with,' says Huy.

'How long can we survive without water?' asks Grace.

'A few days,' says Huy. 'Oh, I hope we don't have to drink the bayou water. It's so dirty.'

'Or the swamp water,' says Grace.

'I hope there's no flesh-eating bacteria in it,' I say. We sit in silence for a while.

'Eliza,' says Avery shakily, 'do you think the ice caps have melted?'

'Those poor polar bears,' says Grace.

'Why do you think that?' I ask.

'Because of all the water. How else can the sea level rise so much overnight?'

'The sea level *is* rising,' I reply. 'But this water's not from the ice caps; it's part of the hurricane. You haven't studied this yet?'

Avery and Grace glance at each other. 'We don't always pay attention in class,' says Avery guiltily.

'It's called a storm surge. The hurricane pushes the ocean water on to the land.'

'Will it go back down again?' asks Grace.

'I hope so.' I look around me. Everything's vanished beneath the waves.

'I can't believe we're stuck on a piece of wood after a hurricane,' says Huy, 'all because of those stupid footprints that I never even believed belonged to the loup-garou. And I lost my accordion.'

Grace and Avery fall silent, watching the waves beneath them.

'You think this is how I expected this night to turn out?' says Avery. 'I thought we were going to discover a new species. I thought we were going to catch a loup-garou and . . .' she pauses and shrugs her shoulders, 'save everything.'

'We did discover something,' I say. 'That sinkhole was real, wasn't it?'

'I saw the squirrel disappear,' says Grace.

Huy nods. 'The sinkhole's real. But that won't help us save anything.'

'What even causes a sinkhole?' asks Avery.

'My dad says it's a salt dome that collapses,' explains Huy. 'Sinkholes sometimes happen naturally but most of the time it's because of an accident.'

'What kind of accident?' I ask.

'When people are drilling for oil they accidentally puncture the side and then water rushes in and dissolves the salt pillars.' He gestures as he describes it.

'I wonder what happened to all those people there in the storm?' I ask.

We stare at each other and into the water around us. Everyone is tired. My body shakes with exhaustion. If I can just keep their spirits up, keep them going . . . they have to be all right.

'Tell us something to take our minds off all of this,' I say. 'Tell us about your trip to Vietnam.' Huy has aunts and uncles there and last year he visited them for the first time.

'Well, Vietnam has the same humidity as here but everything else is different. There's lots more people, cars, motorbikes and bicycles. There was a bay I visited with clear blue water and limestone islands covered in rainforest. We got a boat with orange fanned sails. That was my favourite moment.'

'What about you, Grace?' I ask. 'What's your favourite holiday memory?'

'Bodyboarding in the waves on the beaches of Florida,' she says.

'Avery?' I ask.

'Eating snow cones on the levee with you.'

I smile. 'That's one of my favourites too,' I say, proud that her best memory has me in it and still feeling guilty that I destroyed her shrimping dream. I wonder if we can find something else to do together instead.

'We should take it in turns to sleep,' says Huy.

'I'm not tired,' I lie. 'So everyone else can sleep first.'

They lean against each other, wrapping their arms with each other's. Soon I can hear the familiar gentle snoring from Avery. They're asleep.

The scales of an alligator slink past and my body freezes. But it passes, leaving us alone. 'Thank you,' I whisper after it.

After a few hours, everyone wakes up. They stretch and shield their eyes from the bright sun.

'I need to ask you something,' I say to the others. 'When I fell and broke my arm in the swamp, I thought I felt someone pick me up and save me from the alligator. But Grace and Huy didn't know what I was talking about when I asked. And, Avery, you were stuck in the hole. Do you think I imagined it?' I pause. I've been going over it in my mind while they all slept and I know I have to ask, but even so I feel silly. 'Or do you think . . . Do you think it might have been the loup-garou?' The words hang in the air.

'It was me,' says Grace quietly.

'You picked me up? Why didn't you say?' I ask.

'No, not that.' She takes a deep breath. 'Iwastheloup-garou. Imadethefootprints.' She speaks so fast, spilling her words, that I can hardly understand her.

'I'msorryI'msorryI'msorry,' she says.

'Slow down,' I say. 'What happened?'

'I made the footprints,' she says, quietly and more slowly this time, staring at her hands.

'What?' asks Huy.

'No,' says Avery, scrunching her face. 'I found them with you.'

'I made them to cheer you up, Avery,' Grace says. 'And then I pretended to find them with you.' She turns to me and Huy. 'I didn't think

Avery would want to search for a loup-garou at night and I definitely didn't think she'd disappear. I got scared and I panicked and then the longer it went on, the harder it was to say anything. I kept thinking that we'd find her and that it wouldn't even matter.' Grace blurts this all out at once and then pauses, taking a deep breath. She looks like she's on the verge of tears.

'How could you not tell us that whole time?' I ask.

'It would have helped us find her,' says Huy angrily.

'No,' says Grace. 'I thought about that and it wouldn't have. It was best that we were thinking like Avery was. And Avery was looking for the loup-garou.'

'It's not your fault, Grace,' I say, although my jaw is tight as I fight the rising urge to feel like we're all here because of those stupid footprints. 'You weren't to know all of this was going to happen.'

'You mean all yesterday I was searching for fake prints?' asks Avery, and she starts to laugh.

Grace nods.

Avery's laugh is contagious and soon we're all laughing. I don't even know what's funny but the laughter chases the frustration away from my body and leaves me calmer.

There's another whirring engine sound. I frantically search the sky for the helicopter and raise the tattered flag into the air as high as I can. My muscles ache.

But as it gets louder I realise it's not a helicopter. It's a boat.

CHAPTER TWENTY-SIX

Sinking

The boat roars towards us.

It's Huy's dad's. I recognise it immediately. The one he keeps moored under his house. That's a good sign. It means there can't have been too much damage to town. He spots us and points. I finally lower my aching arm.

Dad's face joins Huy's dad's. Then Mom's pops over the side, with Grace's parents' too. They're all there. They're all right.

Mom practically falls off the boat trying to reach us. Her eyes are puffy and tired. She sniffs and grabs us, burying my face in her hair. I'm wrapped up in the smell of cayenne pepper spice. 'I'm here,' she says. 'You're safe now.' And for the first time since we lost Avery I feel my body relax and I let someone else take charge.

Her skin is salty and sticky from the sweat and the humidity. Dad hugs us next. 'Where have you been?' he asks, clutching my head.

'Your arm,' says Mom as she examines it. 'We need to get you to the hospital.'

'Was it a hurricane?' I ask her.

She nods. 'Instead of slowing down it sped up and strengthened into a category-one hurricane. It hit further down the coast, but caused the storm surge and all this flooding here.'

'Is there anyone else still out here from the search party?' I ask.

'The sheriff made us return before the storm hit,' says Mom. 'I didn't want to.' She glances at Dad. I can tell they argued about it.

Mom cradles Beau Beau in her arms, wraps him in a towel and lays him in the cabin of the boat.

'He'll be all right, won't he?' Avery asks.

'We'll try our best,' says Mom. 'From the way he's breathing he looks like he ingested some water in his lungs.'

Dad steps down into the cabin carrying a first-aid box. He bandages up my arm and ties a new sling. 'We'll be at the hospital soon,' he says. 'Try not to worry.'

'We can't go yet,' I say. 'There are more people in the swamp. We found a sinkhole and there were about thirty workers there. It was right before the storm hit. We have to rescue them.'

Mom and Dad glance at each other. 'You're sure it was a sinkhole?' asks Dad.

Avery nods. 'Grace saw a tree being pulled into it.'

Mom's shaking. 'You lot could have been sucked in.'

'Where?' asks Dad.

'In the east side of the swamp,' I say. 'On Soileron's land.'

Dad crouches in front of me.

Mom glances at me, her eyes worried.

'I'll call the sheriff. After the hospital, a group of us will go and investigate,' Dad says.

I sit in the sterile waiting room of the hospital, clutching my arm. It's strange to be out of the swamp. Everything is so squeaky clean here. I feel out of place. My arm's hurting more and more now that the adrenalin's worn off. Dad had to drive through flooded roads to get us to the nearest hospital, which is way inland. The doctors checked Avery for signs of concussion and said it's nothing too serious but that she needs bed rest and lots of fluids. Then they treated all of us for dehydration while we waited for my X-rays to come back.

'It's a clean fracture of your ulna,' says the doctor when she returns, holding up the X-ray for me to see. 'This bone.' She points to my forearm. 'We'll have to put you in a cast for six weeks. After that you'll be healed and good to go.'

'Which colour would you like your cast?' asks the nurse.

'Green,' I say. The colour of the marshes.

After the storm, there's a quietness outside: a slow kind of heaviness from the high humidity and the heat. Our houses remain standing on their stilts even though I was half expecting them to have all been flattened. The ground underneath them has been replaced by water.

Avery, Grace, Huy and I gather in our living room together, waiting for the adults to return from the swamp and Mom to get back from the vet with Beau Beau.

'Can we decorate your cast?' asks Avery, grabbing a clear container packed full with felt-tip pens from a drawer.

I nod and they all transform my cast into a work of art. Avery paints the sea, bayou and the swamp water. Grace adds an alligator and a pelican. Huy carefully draws cypress, tupelo and oak trees.

'I bet people are still talking about moving,' I say. 'Especially after the storm.'

'I won't go,' says Avery, folding her arms across her chest.

Dad flings the front door open and strides in, returning from the sinkhole. His eyes are dark and stormy.

'Are the workers alive?' I ask.

'They're all fine,' he says. 'Most got to the road before the storm hit and the last few were rescued by helicopter.'

'You saw the sinkhole?' I ask.

He nods, grim-faced. I've never seen him this angry before.

'It's awful. We might have to evacuate. That's why Soileron were telling us to leave, offering us money. They were trying to cover this up, trying to get us to go before we found out about the sinkhole. They drilled through the wall of a salt dome! The company's going to have cough up a lot more money now we know it's their fault.'

I glance at Huy. He'd guessed right.

'We can't let them get away with it,' says Dad.

'But I don't want to leave,' I say. My heart sinks. We went into the swamp last night to find a way to stay, to save it, but now it's looking like the only thing we've done is make it even more certain that we have to move.

'My *chére*, we can work with everything nature throws at us. The water. The hurricanes. It's our way of life. We've always been able to find a way to survive,' says Dad. 'But if a sinkhole is sucking the land up, there's nothing we can do.'

CHAPTER TWENTY-SEVEN
Turtle

'What do we do now?' I ask, digesting the information.

'We wait,' says Avery, shrugging.

And we do. We sit on the balcony together and wait – for the water below to recede, for news about the sinkhole, for Mom to come back with Beau Beau.

'It was a stupid idea to go to the swamp,' says Avery. 'I wish we'd never done it.'

'But then we wouldn't have known about the sinkhole. And that's important,' I say.

Later, after Grace and Huy have left, Mom returns, clutching the plastic cat carrier.

I clasp Avery's hand. 'Is he in there? Is he all right?' My stomach quivers.

Mom smiles and spins the front of the carrier round to face us.

Through the bars I see Beau Beau lift his head at our voices, ears pricked, tail swishing back and forth.

'The vet thought he might have pneumonia but he's going to be just fine.'

Avery and I jump up and encircle the carrier. I poke my fingers through and he licks them with his rough tongue.

Mom empties a box full of shoes and lines it with towels. 'Here,' she says. 'We'll let Beau Beau sleep in this box. He needs a quiet, dark place to recover.'

I gently lift Beau Beau, cradling him in my arms for a moment before lowering him on to the towels.

'What was wrong with him?' I ask.

'The vet says that Beau Beau got water in his chest. They gave him fluids and he perked right up.'

Then Mom cooks gumbo and the house fills with the smell of onions, celery and bell peppers.

Avery sighs loudly and flops down on to the couch next to me.

'What's on your mind, sweetheart?' asks Mom from the stove.

'I thought that if I had a way to prove that this place was special,' says Avery, her shoulders dropping, 'then everyone would have a reason to save it.'

Mom comes over to the couch, wiping her hands on a tea towel, and squeezes between us.

'You don't need to prove a loup-garou exists to convince people that this place is special, sweetie.' Mom strokes Avery's hair. 'This might be the only place where there are legends of a loup-garou, where people sing songs about those folktales and where people gather to listen and dance to them. That says something about our community and culture. And that's something worth fighting for too.'

Mom's words cheer Avery up but my thoughts turn to shrimping. She always said being a shrimper was a special part of our culture too.

What will she say when I tell her I don't want to be a shrimper?

Will she think I don't like our way of life?

I check on Beau Beau and drop fresh water into his mouth with a pipette. I know I have to keep him hydrated.

'His breathing's getting stronger,' I say. 'That's got to be a good sign.'

Mom and Avery murmur in agreement from the couch, but I still feel worried.

The next day, Huy and Grace come over.

'Let's go down to the sea,' says Huy. 'It's safe now.'

Outside, the water level has dropped but not fully receded. The tops of long blades of grass stick out of the water.

We row out to the point where we can see the barrier islands. A brown pelican with a six-foot wing span and feathers like a fan swoops over the water before plunge-diving. It resurfaces, folds its wings back and floats on the water. I can see the outline of a fish in its throat sac, thrashing back and forth. The pelican tips his head back and gulps the fish down in one.

'They look like dinosaurs,' says Avery, following my gaze.

'I agree,' I say.

I notice there are brown dots further along the coastline. Something's been brought in by the tide. I row closer and realise drowned nutria corpses have washed up and are already starting to rot. The smell fills the air. Everything decomposes at an accelerated rate in the humidity.

'Gross,' says Huy.

'Not more dead animals,' says Avery.

We sit in silence and watch the reflections of the sky on the rippling water around us.

'We'd better get back,' I say. 'I don't want anyone to worry about us, and Avery's supposed to be resting.'

As we approach the dock, we see a group of people standing on it. There are raised voices and shouting. I pick out Mom and Dad's silhouettes from the crowd, along with Miss Dolly's. We dock the boat and sprint up to them.

The people from Soileron are back. They're standing on chairs trying to calm the thirty or so angry people gathered.

'If everyone could quiet down we can explain,' says the man.

We reach the back of the crowd just in time to see Mom storm up to them.

Her voice is shaky and she points her finger at them. 'You exposed our family to God knows what and you lied about it. You put my children in danger. You caused the sinkhole and you put our houses at risk. This is your fault.' She speaks through clenched teeth, her voice rising.

The man keeps raising his hand, attempting to interrupt her.

'And instead of telling us about it and paying us compensation, you tried to cover it up, tried to pay us off as if you were giving us some kind of charity,' Mom continues. 'You tried to make yourself look like the good guys and all this time you were just doing it to cover your own tracks.'

'Go, Mom,' whispers Avery.

'Now, we don't want to leave. So if there's any way you can fix this horrendous mess you've created, I'd suggest you do it. This is our little corner of the universe and we're going to fight for it.'

Mom turns and strides away. 'Come on, kids,' she says, beckoning us to go with her.

'Wait!' says the man. 'I've been trying to tell you it's not as bad as we first feared.'

Mom pauses and turns back.

'What do you mean?' asks Dad.

'It was a terrible accident but the sinkhole's not going to get any bigger. The town is safe,' he replies. 'There's only one house that's at risk from it.'

'Which house?' asks Mom.

'Mine's the closest,' says Miss Dolly quietly.

'It is yours,' the woman confirms to Miss Dolly. 'But we'll buy the house and all the land from you so you can move somewhere safe.'

'My house will disappear down the hole?' asks Miss Dolly in disbelief.

'It's unlikely,' says the man. 'But we don't think it's worth the risk at this point.'

'Is there nothing we can do to save it?' I ask.

They all shake their heads.

'What about the swamp and all the animals there?' asks Avery. 'Can't you save them?'

'We really are terribly sorry,' says the lady with another shake of her head.

I picture the trees we saw being sucked into the sinkhole and my heart fills with sadness.

Avery and I stand either side of Miss Dolly, holding her hands. I trace the wrinkles of her palm with my thumb. She's lived in that house her whole life. I can't imagine her anywhere else.

'You can stay with us,' says Mom, resting her hand on Miss Dolly's back.

'I suppose that will have to do,' she says, attempting to smile. She's trying to be positive, but I can tell from her drooping shoulders and deep-set eyes that she's devastated. She's not even speaking in French like normal, as if that's been lost too.

Back at the house, I take a deep breath, leave Avery stroking Beau Beau in our room and join Mom in the kitchen. I can't get shrimping out of my head; the thoughts keep eating away at me, leaving my insides all jumbled. I picture Dad. He's so proud to be a shrimper and to live off the land. I remember how joyful he was, showing me what he did with his life, and imagine how devastated he'll be when I tell him I don't want to do it too. He won't understand. I know he won't get it.

But the thing that I keep circling back to is that I know once everything goes back to normal Mom and Dad'll ask me to go out on the boat with them again.

'Did you always want to be a shrimper?' I ask her.

'Definitely,' she replies. 'Just like my mom. Just like you.'

I flinch at her words and bite my lip and glance away.

She notices. 'Do you still want to be a shrimper?' she asks gently.

'I don't know any more,' I say. 'But I don't want to let you and Dad down.'

'*Chére*, you could never let us down.'

'But you always said how important it was to preserve our way of life.'

'You don't have to be a shrimper to do that.'

I spill everything to her about the turtles and the fish. I don't stop there and suddenly I'm telling her how I'm overwhelmed that the land around me is disappearing.

I hear a creak, and turn. Dad's leaning in the front doorway, head tilted, listening.

'How long have you been there?' I ask.

He looks at me and smiles. 'You know I'd never kill a turtle,' he says. 'If one does get caught in the nets I carefully put it back. They're always alive. That's why we only leave the nets down there for fifty-five minutes. So they don't drown.'

'I know,' I say, noticing the sadness in his eyes that I could ever think of him as a turtle killer.

'I care about this place as much as you do,' he continues.

'I just don't think I can do it,' I say. 'And maybe there's something else I might want to do instead. Sorry, Dad.'

'Don't be sorry,' he says. 'I can't expect you to live the same life as me. You have to find your own current in the ocean. Besides, I'm not making as much money as I used to so it's probably for the best.'

'Whatever you want to do, we'll support you,' says Mom.

Dad walks up and hugs me. 'Love you, Turtle.'

As I hear them say those words a pressure lifts from my chest.

'And we really don't have to move?' I ask Dad.

'Not for now,' he says. 'The land's still sinking. But we've bought ourselves more time. We've survived Katrina. We've survived the oil spill. No one's going to tell us that we have to move. We're going to decide for ourselves. And for now, we're going to stay and fight and do our best to save the land that's left.'

Mom walks into her bedroom and returns clutching an oyster shell. She hands it to me. It's the one Dad found and gave to her. It has a pearl attached to its centre.

'Are you trying to tell me that the world is my oyster, Mom?' I ask, laughing.

'Exactly,' she says, and laughs. 'Who knows? Maybe you'll be the one who figures out how to save the land around here.'

I smile at her. 'Now, that's my real dream.'

CHAPTER TWENTY-EIGHT

Aftermath

After two days of waiting, the water finally recedes fully, leaving behind a mess that needs to be cleaned up. Everyone pitches in clearing the debris.

Avery, Grace, Huy and I go down to the coast to pick up the dead nutria. We fill trash bags full of them. My cast keeps getting in the way and in the end Avery stays by my side to help. After several hours, Grace's dad comes to collect the bags.

We all pause in our work and sit down by the dock in a line, watching the ripples of the water. Grace rests her head on her dad's shoulder.

'I'm proud of the way you lot looked out for each other but you need to think about how your actions affect other people too,' he says, talking about our night in the swamp. 'It's all about taking responsibility.'

'Soileron aren't taking responsibility,' says Grace. 'They tried to cover up their mistakes, didn't they?'

Grace's dad tries not to smile.

'You're right,' says Avery. 'Why don't they have to take responsibility for their actions? For what they've done to the swamp?'

He shrugs. 'That's a good question.'

I glance at Avery. She smiles at me through thin lips and I know she's thinking the same thing as me. We can't let Soileron get away with this.

On our walk back to the house Huy whispers, 'If it was an accident, then why did they try and cover it up?'

'Dad says they were trying to save money,' says Avery.

'Something doesn't feel right to me either.' I press my lips flat, deep in thought. 'We need to find out exactly what happened out there.'

'There might be a clue in the trailer we saw,' says Grace. 'There were loads of files in there.'

'Unless it got sucked down into the sinkhole,' says Huy.

'It's worth checking,' I reply.

'Shouldn't we tell them?' asks Grace.

I shake my head. 'Dad says that there will be an investigation but it could take months or a year. I don't want to wait that long. We live here. Don't we deserve to know what's going on now?'

They all nod.

My heart quickens. I can't believe what I'm about to say, only that I know I have to find out for myself. 'Let's investigate. We'll have to be fast before everyone notices. Our parents will be so angry if they find out.'

'You mean go back to the sinkhole?' asks Huy, crossing his arms. 'That is not a good idea. What if something happens? Didn't you listen to anything Grace's dad just told us?'

'Let's leave a note. That way, if we don't come back they'll know where to find us.'

He frowns and still doesn't look convinced.

'If we tell them they'll never let us go, will they?' I add.

We're all quiet for a second.

'There are no more storms coming, are there?' asks Avery.

I shake my head.

'And we already know the way,' says Grace.

'Let's do this,' says Avery.

Back at our house Avery scribbles a note and I leave it in the bathroom cabinet next to Mom's toothbrush. If we're not back by tonight, she'll find it.

We sneak off to the boat and then to the swamp. I try to ignore the guilt creeping through my body for not telling our parents. I've never disobeyed them this much before. But there's never been anything this important before either.

The marsh is covered in pockets of floodwater, transformed by broken branches and leaves. I barely recognise the route. A flock of ibis stand in the shallow water next to us and I'm relieved to see some life around.

We pass Miss Dolly's house and my chest fills with sadness that she can't live there for ever. As we go deeper into the swamp I see further devastation from the hurricane: trees have fallen like dominoes, there's still water everywhere, and Spanish moss – ripped from the trees – dots the water's surface. There's no one around. It's eerily quiet. Even so, my heart pounds with adrenalin. After everything that happened when we went into the swamp without permission, we can't let anything go wrong this time.

'There's the mobile trailer,' says Grace, pointing ahead. It's surrounded by floodwater but still upright, the windows broken and cracked. I climb out of the boat and inside. It stinks of damp and I wade through puddles, tiny mosquito larvae already swimming in them.

'Let's just grab everything and get out,' I say, looking around at the mess of papers, safety tape and building equipment strewn across the floor. The roar of the storm from the other night fills my ears.

We gather soggy folders. Most of the ink has dripped and run.

'This is all there is,' says Huy, with his arms full.

'It's a start. Maybe we'll find a clue,' says Avery. 'Like when we were searching for the loup-garou.'

Huy groans. 'I don't want to get involved in any of that again.'

'But it's not a mythical creature this time,' I say. 'This is real.'

Though as we leave I can't help but check over my shoulder, just in case a loup-garou is watching.

We make it back to the house without anyone noticing we were gone. Mom and Dad are still out in town, clearing and helping after the storm. I rush and pull down the Post-it note from inside the cabinet. We lay the papers on our beds and sift through them. It's pages of diagrams and drawings that I don't understand and a few addresses of people and businesses I don't know.

'There's nothing here,' says Huy after ten minutes. 'It's pointless.'

I sigh and stare around me at the mess of papers, disappointed.

'Wait,' says Grace, holding up a plastic sleeve with a small USB flash drive in the bottom-right corner. 'Maybe there's something on this.'

'Where did you find that?' I ask, examining it. It's damp but doesn't look damaged.

'In this folder,' Grace replies, holding up the outside of it for me to see.

The label says REPORTS in printed letters.

Huy shrugs. 'Could be anything.'

'I'll get Mom and Dad's laptop,' I reply.

'Better be quick,' says Avery, jumping up. 'They could be back any second.'

I rush to the living room and scan the couch, the table, Dad's chair. The laptop's not there. It's not in their bedroom either and I panic that it's in the truck or with Mom and Dad. At last I spot it on the kitchen counter, a recipe for crawfish étouffée still on the screen from the last time Dad used it.

I carry it into the bedroom and we gather round as Grace inserts the USB drive.

The drive is filled with documents. I click a few open and scroll through tables of numbers and data. I have no idea what any of it means and I close them all, feeling hopeless again.

'Try that one,' says Huy, pointing at a document titled GEOPHYSICAL SURVEY.

I read the first lines and my heart flutters.

Côteville Site Map. Geophysical survey for drilling.

Below is a chunk of thick text filled with technical terms I don't understand.

'What on earth does that mean?' asks Avery, squinting at the screen.

We all shake our heads.

I scroll through twenty pages until the very last one, and there, right at the bottom, are the words:

Conclusion: Côteville area unstable for drilling.

We glance at each other. 'They knew,' I whisper in disbelief. 'They were warned not to drill but they did it anyway.'

'And we have proof!' replies Avery.

'You're right,' I say excitedly. Now we know the real reason they were trying to cover the sinkhole up. It was an accident that should never have happened.

Grace jumps up and down on her tiptoes.

'I knew there was more than what they were saying,' says Huy.

'But what do we do now?' I ask. 'We don't even understand most of what that report says.'

'My cousin's a geologist,' says Grace. 'She studies these things: rocks and stuff. I could ask her?'

Grace disappears to ring her cousin as we continue to read through the report, trying to make sense of it. A few minutes later Grace bursts back into the room.

'My cousin says she thinks that we're right. Soileron must have ignored the report. She said if we send it to her she can read through it and help us build a case against them.'

'We figured it out,' I say, and I know I should feel happy. But my excitement quickly fades and my forehead puckers as I fill with anger. Soileron were warned a sinkhole might be created and they chose to drill anyway. Even though they knew the risks. I clench my hand and hold it up to my chest.

How dare they treat this land like it's nothing.

CHAPTER TWENTY-NINE

Spoonbills

Huy slouches over on the bed and sighs, deflated.

'It's awful,' I say.

'It's not just that,' Huy replies.

And then I remember his dad works at Soileron.

'You're worried about your dad?' I ask.

'He didn't have anything to do with this, did he?' asks Avery softly.

'Of course not!' Huy says defensively. He slumps back against the bed frame. 'My dad works on the old pipes to make sure they're still safe to use. He loves this land. He'll be devastated if someone did something on purpose to risk it. To risk us.'

'Let's not say anything until we're sure what's happening,' says Grace. 'My cousin told me it could be months before there's any progress with a case anyway.'

The front door bangs as Mom and Dad return. I quickly slide the laptop, folders and papers under my pillows just before Dad pops his head around the door. 'Want a snack?' he asks.

We all nod. And he disappears again.

'How are we supposed to fight to save the land when even the big companies won't?' I ask, speaking quietly so Mom and Dad don't hear.

'We make sure that we can do it without them,' says Huy.

'How?' I reply.

'We have to come up with our own ideas for how to do things. Like the people in my wildlife magazines are always doing. They study things and run tests and experiments and stuff to see what works,' says Avery, picking a magazine up off the floor and flicking through it. 'Like this article is about a woman who studies the shrinking ice caps to try and help the polar bears. It says she's an ecologist. What's that?'

Dad returns with carrot sticks and cookies and places them on the chest of drawers before leaving.

'Someone who studies the environment and the animals and plants that live in it,' says Huy in a matter-of-fact tone as he reaches for a cookie.

'You're right,' I say to Avery, standing up. 'If we want to arm ourselves with everything we need to fight against the sinking land, we've got to learn all about the floating marshlands, the swamps and the ecosystems.'

I think about how they exist in a delicate balance and need all the extra protection that they can get.

'Yes!' say Grace and Avery, and they put their hands together in the middle and look up expectantly at me and Huy.

'Er,' I say, glancing at Huy, who's crossed his arms. 'Maybe let's just make a promise to do everything to save the land,' I add, feeling too old for a team hand stack now. It makes what we're doing feel like a game, but this is serious.

'Fine,' says Avery sulkily, but as I glance at her I catch her grinning, teasing me.

'We promise,' they both say.

Next day, to celebrate the end of the storm, the town holds a *fais do-do* – a party.

As I walk there past the dock, I notice the clumps of yellowing marsh grass dying, the drowned trees and the disappearing coastline. For the first time I see the subtle changes as warning signs, our last chance to save the wetlands before they're lost for ever.

The rhythmic music of an accordion, fiddle, guitar and washboard fills the yard as I arrive. The Cajun band plays while people gather and eat jambalaya.

I weave between groups, overhearing snippets of conversations. Everyone is talking about the sinkhole.

Pink spoonbills fly across the bright-blue sky in a v-shape. It reminds me that the migratory birds will soon be arriving. Louisiana is the first place where they can stop and rest after flying across the Gulf. And in spring and fall, they swoop from the sky, filling the trees, marshes and grasslands, recovering from their long journeys over the ocean.

My thoughts turn to the time we watched a small yellow bird drop out of the sky into the water. We rescued it and brought it to land. I didn't think much of it then, but now I realise that as the land disappears, they have to fly further and further to reach a stopping point on their migration. That little bird was too exhausted to make it.

'I've lived here all my life. I'm not going to turn my back on it,' says Grace's dad as I pass.

I reach the serving table and fill my bowl with the smoked sausage, chicken and rice jumbalaya.

'Remember our promise?' Avery pats me on the shoulder.

I nod and smile. 'Of course.'

I think about how we vowed to learn about the land beneath our feet, to be able to stop this kind of thing from happening in the future. And maybe even discover a way to fix it.

Huy approaches and holds out his hand to me.

'Can I have this dance?' he asks. 'I'll be extra careful of your cast.'

'Yes,' I reply, and with my good arm I take his hand.

Grace and Avery whizz past us, dancing together too.

The yard is filled with people bopping and pirouetting. As a waltz begins, everyone moves in a circle together and dances. Huy spins me round and round, laughing. My curls fly out behind me.

Mom and Dad sway and turn next to us, gazing into each other's eyes.

The musicians switch back and forth between French and English in their lyrics.

The sun sets and pelicans dip in and out of the bayou.

I glance round at everyone and am proud of our home and our community. I know in my heart that even with the encroaching water, we can find a way to live alongside the sea, to hold back the waves and to stop the land from sinking.

EPILOGUE

Three months later

'The new net's arrived,' says Dad. 'Want to help me attach it? You can help too, Avery.'

She beams. We carry the net down to the dock together with Beau Beau prancing behind us, tail sticking straight up into the air. The net's fitted with a special device to stop turtles and fish getting caught. We hold the green netting steady while Dad attaches it to *Whippersnapper*.

Avery climbs to the helm and rubs her hand over her name, which is newly engraved on the steering wheel. I told Mom that it didn't feel right without Avery's name on it. Beau Beau jumps on the deck, stretches and yawns, before curling up and wrapping his long tail around his body.

The shrimping season opens again soon and Mom and Dad will be back out there working.

I stare out over the marshland at a great blue heron, standing statue-like. The water's crept a little closer but everything else looks the same. We made it through another hurricane season. The houses are still standing.

Huy walks alongside us, tufts of long grass tucked under his arms. He's helping to plant smooth cordgrass along the coast. It stabilises the soil and stops it from washing away. They plant them in staggered rows, three feet apart.

'A baby step in the right direction,' Mom had called it.

It's one of the many things that holds our patchwork of land together. We're fighting this battle together.

Because if we go, the land won't be the only thing that vanishes under the waves. It will be our communities, the animals, the plants.

All gone.

'Eliza!' shouts Grace, running down to the dock. 'Avery!'

I straighten and spin round.

'Guesswhatguesswhatguesswhat?' she says as she reaches us. 'Soileron are accepting responsibility and settling. They're giving the land back to us as a gift and turning it into a wildlife sanctuary. And Miss Dolly's house might be safe in the future.' Grace continues talking about Miss Dolly's house but the words wash over me. The important thing is that we're in charge of the land now. That means no one can harm the creatures and plants there.

'Saving the land is my number-one mission,' says Avery.

'Even over shrimping?' I ask her.

She nods.

I smile. We have a new shared dream. Like shrimping, it's part of our way of life, but this goal is ours. It's one we both care about. One we can do together.

Author's note

I met my husband in India in 2012 and over the past few years we've spent much time in his hometown in Louisiana, where I was first introduced to the communities in Acadiana. While conducting research for this story, I discovered that Louisiana is losing, on average, a football field sized amount of land into the Gulf of Mexico every hour and that the Governor has declared a state of emergency over the disappearing coastline.

I experienced the rising waters for myself when my friend Sarah and her parents, Brent and Debbie Fanguy, kindly took me to their house, only accessible by a boat through the wetlands and now raised sixteen feet above ground. Along the way, Brent pointed out the places he camped as a child that have now completely vanished under water.

Later that day, Brent's father, Julius, told me stories of the *rougarou*, the word in the local dialect for the *loup-garou*, and how several times as a child he thought he saw one. These Cajun words originated with the French Acadians,

French speaking people who settled in Canada, then migrated to Louisiana in the 18th century.

The loss of coast leaves the land vulnerable to storms and threatens many coastal communities too. With its alligators, turtles and swamps, these wetlands are a truly unique wilderness. Despite the land loss, there's hope, with different solutions working together, that it's not too late to save them.

Acknowledgements

There are many people who have taken the time to help me with this book and I'm forever grateful to all of you.

A special thank you to Lena McCauley, my wonderful editor, who was instrumental in every step of this writing process, from idea conception to line edits. This book was very much a joint effort and I'm so thankful to have shared it with you.

To everyone at Orion Children's Books and Hachette Children's Group. Thank you for everything! You are a brilliant and inspiring team to be a part of.

To my fantastic agent, Sallyanne Sweeney. Thank you!

To Rob Biddulph, thank you for designing and illustrating the beautiful cover. It's perfect.

To the Society of Authors, who awarded me a grant which enabled me to carry out the research behind this book.

To Joshua Caffery, whose gorgeous poem is the foreword to this story, from his collection of poems and songs from Louisiana folklore, *In the Creole Twilight*.

To John Oliver, who brought the setting to life by drawing the beautiful map.

To Sarah, Brent and Debbie Fanguy for showing me the marsh and the wetlands and sharing their knowledge of the water. To John, Jonathan and Huy for accompanying me on my research adventures.

To Katie Cummings, who answered all my geological questions and taught me about sinkholes.

To Scott Jones for teaching me about the ecology of the coast and why the land is sinking into the sea.

To Dan Kennison and Jonathan Jarret for sharing their stories of the Louisiana outdoors.

To Clélie Ancelet for helping with the French.

To Sarah and Jennifer, my workshop group. Thank you!

To Rick Herrmann, who very aptly named Monsieur Beau Beau.

To Anne deMahy Herrmann, for all your love, support, and inspiration with writing and in life. Thank you!

To my sisters: Rachel, Olivia and Hazel Butterworth and Emily Kennison; my mum Anya Berry; and my gran Mary Roche. I'm proud to have such feisty women in my life.

To my husband Jonathan Kennison, for sharing your love of your home and the swamps, your childhood stories, and for teaching me how to dance.

To all the educators, teachers, librarians, and booksellers. Thank you!

And finally to my readers, a huge thank you for embarking on the journey with these characters. Keep adventuring and exploring, whether it's in real life or through the books you get lost in.

Also by

JESS BUTTERWORTH

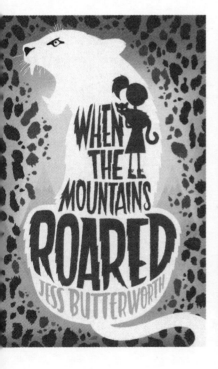